LIN CARTER,
MASTER OF FANTASY,

has produced in his World's End novels
a *most amazing and complex creation.*

Here is Ganelon Silvermane, the mighty
warrior who was intended by his ancient de-
signers to be the world's Last Hero.

Here is the legendary Flying City, self-
contained, self-directed, and seeking only inhabitants to fill its luxurious houses.

Here is the world's oldest man, the dis-
coverer of immortality, who had probably
forgotten more science in his thousands of
years than any then living ever knew.

Here is an all-star cast of marvelous people
from the varied days of the dying sun's set-
ting on the Last Continent of a doomed planet.

Lin Carter

THE IMMORTAL OF WORLD'S END

DAW BOOKS, INC.
DONALD A. WOLLHEIM, PUBLISHER

1301 Avenue of the Americas
New York, N. Y.   10019

For Ken (or Ben) Sano, of
Albany, who enjoys this
sort of thing.

FIRST PRINTING, SEPTEMBER 1976

1 2 3 4 5 6 7 8 9

PRINTED IN U.S.A.

Contents

Book One:

DEFENDERS OF VALARDUS

Book Two:

SILVERMANE AT ZARADON

Book Three:

THE MAD EMPIRE OF TRANCORE

Book Four:

AGAINST THE XIMCHAKS

Book One

DEFENDERS OF VALARDUS

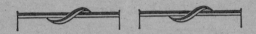

The Scene: The Mobile City of Kan Zar Kan; the Purple Plains; the border of Greater Zuavia; the Kingdom of Valardus.

The Characters: Ganelon Silvermane, Xarda of Jemmerdy, Prince Erigon, Grrff the Xombolian; a Gynosphinx, a magician, a machinist; citizens of Kan Zar Kan and Valardus; Ximchak Barbarians.

1.

Kan Zar Kan Moves North

From horizon to horizon there stretched a flat and featureless prairie of thick, lush grass. This verdure ranged in hue from lavender and purple to deep violet, but for the most part the plain was covered with grasses of purple hue. For this reason it was known to the geographers of Gondwane the Great, the last and by far the mightiest of the continents of Old Earth, as the Purple Plains.

One afternoon early in the spring of a year some seven hundred million years in the future of our own time, there might have been observed traversing these Purple Plains a vehicular contrivance of unusual proportion and design. On a huge metal dishlike base rose a crest of towers, spires, domes, and less easily defined structures; all were constructed of a glittering and highly polished metal, and in accordance to nonhuman canons of architectural design, so that the truncated domes and circular ziggurats resembled nothing more than so many immense Christmas-tree ornaments.

The enormous metallic contrivance, which was as large as a fair-sized town, negotiated the Purple Plains by riding an air cushion generated by whirring rotor blades situated beneath its base. All in all, a most unusual vehicle.

The Mobile City of Kan Zar Kan (as it was called) had been originally designed as a self-propelled metals mine, with ore refineries and machine shops built in, the whole maintained by an artificial intelligence of considerable intellectual capacity and remarkable tenacity of purpose. Equipped with subelectronic senses able to detect buried deposits of metal ore, the mammoth robot had originally cruised the Plains, squatting above such deposits while its extensible drills plundered the lode. Then, while the robot refineries processed the raw ore into finished ingots, the robot mine decamped for other promising sites.

The giant perambulating robot had been devised by an extinct civilization called Vandalex, which had collapsed some ten million years before the period of this story. And when the robot brain realized in time that no further airships were likely to visit it in order to relieve it of its stockpiled ingots, it retooled its factories to another purpose. By its electronic sensories, Kan Zar Kan noticed neighboring cities more or less of a size with itself: modifying its design to resemble, rather haphazardly, such centers of human and nonhuman populace, the Mobile City became adept at capturing mercantile caravans, emigrations, parties of pilgrims, and other groups of humanity en route, for one purpose or another, across the Purple Plains.

Its most recent captive populace, a ragtag band of gypsy tinkers called Iomagoths, had at length come to an agreement of sorts with Kan Zar Kan, and soon the Mobile City would realize its fondest dreams and become an actual city—the sort of city, that is, which remains permanently in one place, with genuine citizens and so on.

It had been Ganelon Silvermane and his friends who had been instrumental in bringing the City and its tatterdemalion citizenry together in amicable accord. In gratitude for their services in this regard, the former chief of the Iomagoths, now the First King of Kan Zar Kan, King Yemple by name, had instructed the City to bear Ganelon and his friends north into Greater Zuavia, toward the Kingdom of Valardus, their destination. The City was only too happy to oblige. It had gotten along fairishly on its own steam, intellectually speaking, but was inordinately pleased to have a capable human hand on the throttle. For the past several days, then, the mobile metal metropolis had traveled steadily north, crossing the vast immensities of the Purple Plains which formed the border between two enormous conglomerates of nations and city-states, Northern YamaYamaLand and Greater Zuavia.

On this particular afternoon, Ganelon and his associates were enjoying the mellow sunlight and brisk, spanking breeze on the upper tier of the Red Ziggurat, an imposing structure at the center of the City which housed the instrumentality of the City Brain and had, more recently, become the Royal

Palace of King Yemple and his teenaged daughter, Princess Slioma.

Leaning against the rail, Xarda, a knightrix of Jemmerdy, gazed northward dreamily, while Prince Erigon of Valardus stood beside her. The two young people formed a striking contrast in types, and an unusual reversal of roles. That is, while Prince Erigon was a good-looking young man with an affable expression, he was a trifle languid and slight of build, looking more like a scholar, with his well-formed and noble expanse of brow, or a poet, with his large, dreamy eyes and delicate features framed in long, curled hair, than a man of action.

This was, in fact, very largely the case.

The girl at his side, however, for all her youth, was striking in a vivid, vigorous, warlike sort of way. She had carelessly tousled curls of burning red, and bright, keen green eyes, a small snub nose boyishly sprinkled with freckles, a wide, grinning mouth, and a small, adorably stubborn chin.

Her clothing, what little of it there was, could not have been described, by any stretch of the imagination, as feminine. Indeed, all she wore were odds and ends of burnished steel armor: steel breastplates cupped the firm rondures of her shallow, adolescent bosom; greaves and buskins were strapped to her long, lissom legs; an abbreviated kilt shielded her tummy and upper thighs from a chance swordstroke, and this brief garment was made of strips of tough leather, washed in silver gilt and studded with rivets of steel.

A thick-bladed and businesslike dagger was sheathed at her upper left thigh. Against the other, a slim, deadly longsword was scabbarded. In all, she resembled an adolescent Amazon.

Xarda of Jemmerdy, however, despite her military appearance, was a healthy young girl of perfectly normal emotions. In her small and rather distant country it was the custom for the men to attend to the scholarly, artistic, intellectual, philosophical, scientific, and administrative forms of human endeavor, while the women, organized in nine knightly fellowships, took care of such matters as war, adventure, police, and civil defense.

As a Sirix of Jemmerdy, the girl knight was perfectly at home in a swordfight or a siege, preferred derring-do to dusting, conquest to cookery, and would far rather mop up a dastardly band of desperadoes than the floor.

The young Prince at her side, she thought, rather resembled the foppish, artistic male aristocracy of her native realm. Actually, this was quite unfair to Erigon of Valardus. While the amiable and good-natured young Prince was fond of books and poetry, he was hardly at a loss when it came to cut-and-thrust. The women of his homeland customarily attended to their housewifery, leaving the men to run everything else, including the wars. The trouble with Valardus, however, was that until very recently it had enjoyed an unprecedented and uninterrupted period of peaceful calm which had endured for so many generations that the knightly or martial arts had all but atrophied through sheer disuse and neglect. For this reason, when his country was threatened with imminent invasion by a vast Horde called the Ximchak Barbarians, his father, Good King Vergus, despairing of the military ignorance prevalent among the current generation of Valardine males, had dispatched him on a mission south to recruit some mercenaries.

This mission had come to grief. Imprisoned in Chx, Erigon had met two stalwart and doughty warriors, however, who had agreed to accompany him north to Valardus. Two warriors alone, you might think, had little hope of breaking the siege of Valardus. So, at least, you might presume. But then you have not met Ganelon Silvermane and his comrade-in-arms, Grrff the Karjixian.

Silvermane had been raised in Zermish, one of the cities of the Hegemony, and while little more than a boy he had broken the ferocious Indigons at the Battle of Uth, in which action he had won his Agnomen. He had been educated by a powerful and somewhat mysterious enchanter called the Illusionist of Nerelon, and had thence embarked on a career of wandering, adventuring, and errantry.

Still in his first youth, the towering bronze giant topped seven feet by several inches. The breadth of his shoulders, the deep chest, the massive arms, were truly herculean. His grim, heavy-jawed, somber face, with its black and scowling brows, made him seem formidable. Actually, Ganelon was a pleasant, mannerly young fellow—mild-tempered, easygoing, little given to speech.

His most impressive single feature (once you had gotten used to his heroic height and tremendous physique) was his unshorn mane of sparkling and metallic hair the color of spun silver: the identical hue of the five-foot broadsword scabbarded between his gigantic shoulders. This inhuman banner of silver hair (from which derived his Agnomen, Silvermane) marked him for a nonhuman. He was, in fact, a Construct, an artificial superman, an android bred for some unguessable mission by an extinct race called the Time Gods.

The weapon he bore was called the Silver Sword; and it was enchanted.

While a captive of the Queen of Red Magic, Ganelon had fallen in with Grrff of Xombol, and the two were fast friends by now. Grrff was a nonhuman, a member of a warlike race called the Tigermen of Karjixia. One look at his flat skull, whiskery black muzzle, impressive fangs, fierce but friendly yellow eyes, tufted ears, and burly-chested, heavy-shouldered body, with its black-barred orange fur tending to white on chest, belly, and loins, and you would have understood why his race was called Tigermen.

A noted warrior in his own right, Grrff was of the Farrowl clan of Xombol. Because of his natural coat of fur, he required no other clothing save for a girdle of green leather which supported his ygdraxel, a black leather groincup, and leather gloves studded with steel spikes. He and Ganelon had escaped together from the Red Enchantress of Shai, and had shared several adventures ere now.

But none, perhaps, quite as odd as that which would very soon befall. . . .

The two warriors were discussing the fine points of barroom brawling, gutter-tumble, and knife-to-knife combat when a calm, pleasant, artificial voder-voice interrupted them; it was broadcast by loudspeakers set up all over the City, and represented the voice of Kan Zar Kan.

"Attention, all citizens and guests . . . this is your City speaking. . . . Aerial visitants are approaching from the north, and, in view of this, tonight's fireworks display and street picnic are postponed until further notice. Please take cover in my conveniently marked Civil Defense Shelters. . . . The aerial attack will commence in two minutes, thirty-four seconds."

2.

Visitors From Above

Startled by the announcement, Grrff jumped, swore, snatched out his ygdraxel, and stared about the four quarters of the sky, furry ears bristling.

"My Claws and Whiskers," the Tigerman swore in his hoarse, deep-chested voice, "I don't see anything! What about you, big man?"

Ganelon had unsheathed the Silver Sword and held it at the ready, his eyes prowling the heavens. Suddenly he elevated one huge arm, pointing.

"There, off that way. A flying object—"

Xarda came swaggering up, longsword ready, eyes bright.

"By my Halidom, can it be outriders of the Horde?" the girl knight demanded belligerently. "My steel is thirsty and could do with a modicum of practice, s'truth!"

Prince Erigon came strolling up in the rear, an interested expression on his pleasant features. His heraldic blazon, woven in thread of silver and purple enamel on his courtly tabard, caught the sunlight, glittering like mail.

"Oh, I say, are we in for a bit of a fight?" he inquired mildly, glancing about. Xarda snorted scornfully at the languid tone in which he spoke, but Ganelon noticed with approval that Erigon's hand was on the pommel of his rapier, which he could handle with easy familiarity, and that neither his voice nor his manner displayed trepidation.

By this time the flying thing had come considerably closer, and was beginning to descend over the City, weaving between the sharp metal spires. They could make out something of its nature by this point, and it proved surprising. Probably they had expected something in the nature of a flying machine or an artificial aerial contrivance of some kind, like Istrobian's flying kayak, which was the sky vessel used by Prince Erigon.

This was no flying machine, however, but a winged beast.

"I say," said Erigon interestedly, "I believe the creature is a sphinx!"

And so, indeed, it appeared to be. Thrice the size of any ordinary lion, yet lionlike in its catlike form, clad in tawny, sand-colored fur, the curious feline had broad, feathered wings which sprang from immense shoulder muscles just behind the joint of the forelimbs. These wings were dark brown, like those of the extinct and now-legendary eagle, but the feathers were tipped with gold. Golden, too, was the thick, curly mane which curled over the neck and about the shoulders in a thoroughly lionlike manner.

Xarda noted a further detail, and cleared her throat.

"Ahem!" she observed. "I believe *Gynosphinx* would be the more accurate term." Ganelon followed the direction of her gaze, and colored. But Xarda was certainly right; the sphinx was indeed a female, for from her broad chest swelled huge breasts, tawny-white of skin, with bright-pink nipples like the dugs on the mammaries of a brood-cow.*

The Gynosphinx was truly immense, almost fifteen feet long; her wings, when fully extended, measured thirty-two feet from tip to tip. Her curly-maned head was as big as a barrel, with a broad-cheeked, flat face, huge eyes of glowing green under a low brow, a flat nose, and a wide, lipless mouth filled with blunt, tusklike fangs. The features were similar to those of a human female, but broadened and flattened and distorted, and the nose was blunt and flat like a muzzle, but devoid of whiskers.

Grrff gawped skyward, fascinated. Long separated from the females of his kind, the Tigerman found the Gynosphinx entrancing, if a trifle intimidating. She was two and a half times his own weight, and, had she been capable of mating, could probably have snapped his spine or crushed his ribcage in the frenzy of her coupling.

"Gadzooks, the beast is tame!" swore Xarda, incredulously.

They looked and saw what she meant. Mounted astride

---

*The sphinx is not only sterile and cannot be bred but lacks the organs of gender. The genus exists in two distinct species, the Androsphinx, which is bearded and nominally male, and the Gynosphinx, which is ostensibly female. Ishgadara was a Gynosphinx.

the broad back of the winged women-headed lion were two
riders.

One was tall and skinny, his bony form wrapped in flow-
ing robes of mystic purple, adorned with astrological sym-
bols embroidered in heavy gold thread. His visage was vague
and his manner absent-minded, but good-natured and amiable. He had a long white beard and a smooth, unwrinkled
face whose seeming youthfulness belied his apparent age. In
one hand he carried an ivory wand tipped with a griffin's
claw in worked gold, clutching a large smoky yellow diamond.
From time to time the glowing aura of the gem waxed
and waned.

Seated behind him, clutching the tall man about the waist
with pudgy arms, rode a very short, very fat little man with
a round red face with fat cheeks and indignant, china-blue
eyes and a huge, ferocious-looking pair of mustachios.
The little fat man was dressed in a tattered smock of dull-
brown cloth, scorched here and there with acid burns, and
stained with chemicals where it was not scorched. He was
completely bald save for a fluffy fringe of snowy, bristling
hair which tufted above his ears and around the back of his
head like a monkish tonsure.

Whoever these two uninvited visitors from above might
prove to be, they did not look very warlike or particularly
threatening.

The huge Gynosphinx settled to the surface of the tier
as gently as a fluttering leaf. The two dismounted and stared
about them while their enormous mount folded her broad
wings and began to groom her breast and paws, licking with
an immense pink tongue, for all the world like an ordinary
pussycat.

The tall, bearded man straightened his purple robes absently, peering about in an interested, but inattentive, manner. The fat red-faced man, observing that they were observed, tried vainly to detract his attention from whatever it
was he was thinking about, gave up, and came waddling over
on short fat legs.

"Your pardon, sirs and madam, for this untimely intru-
sion, but me colleague and I—" he began, in a wheezing
voice.

The tall skinny man, who had been peering with near-
sighted interest at anything and everything, turned his gaze
on Grrff, and spoke up so suddenly behind the fat little man
that the fat man jumped.

"Oh, I say, Ollub! A Tigerman! From Karjixia?" he inquired, strolling toward where the burly, furry warrior stood, clutching his ygdraxel, licking his whiskers nervously.

Grrff indicated that Karjixia was indeed his home.

"Quite so, quite so, I'm sure," murmured the taller of the two. Clasping his hands together behind his back, he strolled around and around the Tigerman, examining him with dreamy interest, as if he were a work of art.

"You must pardon the manners o' Palensus Choy," puffed the fat, red-faced man. "I believe he were instrumental in assisting the Tigermen of Karjixia to evolve from they feline ancestry some forty thousand year ago—"

"Fifty," said the tall man, whose name appeared to be Choy.

"Fifty, then. He takes, as be only natural, a scientific interest in the outcome of his experiments," continued the fat man apologetically.

"Not scientific, thaumaturgic," corrected Choy absently. "And they are not experiments, but projects. Tell me, my good fellow," he addressed Grrff abruptly, "do you breed true?"

The Xombolian blinked dazedly, then shrugged.

"I have not been able to breed recently," he said in his deep, hoarse voice, with a little growling laugh, "but when last I found myself with my female, and she in heat, cubs were the outcome of our affections, as is usually the case. A litter of eight ensued, I believe. . . ."

"Quite so, quite so," mused Palensus Choy.

"Might one inquire, sir, as to your own cognomen?" asked Prince Erigon politely. The short man jerked an ungainly bow, and introduced himself as Ollub Vetch, machinist.

"Too modest, my dear fellow, too modest," murmured Choy, flapping a bony hand at his companion. "The distinguished Vetch, you should know, is a renowned inventor, experimentalist, and savant of the physical sciences—"

"While me colleague," puffed Vetch, with a cheerful grin, "be none other than the celebrated magician Palensus Choy, of Zaradon, a savant of the, ahem, *para*physical sciences, if so I may term the discipline of applied mysticism!"

"Not the famous 'Immortal of Zaradon,' surely!" exclaimed Prince Erigon.

"Tush," murmured Choy modestly. His colleague, however, was not so modest.

"Indeed so," he wheezed. A scornful grimace distorted his

plump and rubicund features, and he said disdainfully: "As
much as it pains me to lend credence to the pitiful delusions
of so-called 'magicians,' I believe himself devoted the first few
centuries o' his novitiate to the Secret of Immortality, which
magisterium he claims to have mastered. Since his longevity
has, thus far, extended to the inordinate length of some six
and one-half million years, I suppose ye could claim his
work in that area to have been, more of less, successful."

Grrff turned a curious, almost awe-filled gaze upon the tall
figure of the absent-minded magician. Then he went over to
where Ganelon Silvermane stood, leaning on the Silver
Sword, and whispered hoarsely in his ear.

"If yonder fellow is who he claims to be, then he is the
Father of my Race, and a supermagician of enormous
power," he breathed.

"To have lived to the age of six and one-half million
years," replied Silvermane seriously, "one would have to be a
magician of considerable power. Is he a friendly magician,
though? Some of them are, and some of them are not."

The Tigerman shrugged dubiously.

Xarda went straight to the point without beating about
the bush, as was usually her way.

"What are you doing here, magister?" she demanded. "Do
you mean us harm, or do you come as a friend?"

"Oh, my purposes are friendly enough, I suppose, my
dear," said Palensus Choy offhandedly. "The city of Valardus
is under seige by the most enormous herd of ruffians imag-
inable, you know. My enchanted palace, Zaradon, lies not
far north, and my guest and I decided to investigate the
matter at first hand, so to speak. Crystals are notoriously un-
reliable, you know; never manage to grind the things to
optical perfection, I fear. Observed this curious self-propelled city-machine of yours approaching from the south, and
thought we had best take a look at you, too. Do you come
to aid the ruffians, or the poor Valardines?"

"The Valardines, Galendil willing," said Xarda in a posi-
tive tone.

"Splendid, splendid. . . . Ah, this contrivance of yours—
Vandalexian, I believe?"

Ollub Vetch bristled at this.

"Of course, Vandalex, ye skinny fool!" snapped the little
red-faced fat man. "A superb example o' technology at its
most triumphant."

"Ah, to be sure," murmured Choy absently. Then, with a

vague smile to Xarda, he murmured in explanation: "I fear my pudgy colleague and I are constantly at variance over the respective excellences of scientific machinery and sorcerous magics!"

Just then a nervous, dirty-faced boy in tattered gypsy finery poked his nose around a doorway. It was, Ganelon saw, an Iomagothic boy called Kurdi. Yemple had recently taken the little ragamuffin for his page—once it had been explained to him that all kings had pages, that is.

"Yes, what is it, Kurdi? Don't be shy, these are friends— I think," said the bronze giant, reassuringly.

"K-k-king Y-y-yemple, he say—" stuttered the gypsy boy.

"Yes?" asked Ganelon encouragingly.

"H-he s-say, is we invaded, er what?"

"No, we're not. These are just visitors."

"In th-that c-case," hissed the boy, "l-lunch be served."

"I say! Did someone mention 'lunch'?" demanded Palensus Choy pertly, displaying for the first time a sharp and alert interest.

So they all trooped in to lunch.

3.

The Siege in Stalemate

Luncheon was served in the new Royal Feasting Hall, which had formerly been a subassembly plant and whose concrete floor still bore mute testimony to its former plebeian purpose in the form of oilstains and graphite smudges.

King Yemple presided over the festivities. He was an enormous fat man with more chins and cheeks and tummies than it seemed could be fitted onto one human frame, and sharp black shrewd eyes that never missed a trick. His portly person was wrapped in gaudy garments of royal purple, imperial crimson, and lots and lots of gold—gold lace, gold buttons, gold medals, and gold jewelry.

Now that he was reassured that they were not, after all, being invaded, his genial sense of hospitality became expansive, even lavish. He pressed additional helpings on his guests until even the fat little inventor confessed himself unable to down another bite.

Palensus Choy, however, was made of sterner stuff. Lean as a rail, the absent-minded magician had a truly gargantuan appetite and was capable of putting away enough nutriment to satisfy any three ordinary men.

"Do he'p yersef ta s'more a these here tasty morsels, me lord Choy," the gypsy monarch grinned obsequiously. Nodding vigorously, and mumbling something about "juicy tidbits," the skinny magician shoveled a few dozen more of the greasy gobbets of shishkabob onto his platter.

" 'Juicy tidbits,' eh?" chuckled Grrff, in a *sotto voce* comment to Zilth, the scrawny, rat-faced little rogue who was currently serving the Kan Zar Kanian court in the capacity of Prime Minister, Privy Councilor, and First Lord of the Admiralty. "I wonder what yonder skinny ol' geezer would say if he knew he wuz eating skewered and broiled sewer rat?"

Zilth sniffed and observed the grinning Tigerman through his monocle in an affected manner.

"Ill-mannered lout," he sniffed in a superior accent.

"What's that?" growled Grrff, bristling. It had not been too long since that this same posturing Prime Minister had been a whining, sniveling guttersnipe, whimpering under Grrff's heavy paw, and the Xombolian had trouble adjusting to the new state of affairs.

Zilth squeaked, paled, and ducked. Then, remembering himself, and the dignity of his high position, he stiffened. "It be High Treason ta th' Crown, fellow, ta liff yer hand against th' Prime Minnyster," he reminded the Tigerman.

Grrff relaxed, chuckling.

"I'll prime your minister for you, Zilth you rogue, if you put on airs with ol' Grrff," he rumbled warningly, but without really meaning it.

His heart really wasn't in quarreling with the likes of Zilth, anyway. Grrff was fascinated by the Gynosphinx, whose name was Ishgadara. Palensus Choy had explained that she was fully intelligent, capable of human speech, and would behave herself indoors. So Yemple, in his hearty come-one, come all way, invited her to luncheon, too.

She had just lapped up enough meat stew and gravy out of a bathtub-sized salver, solid gold studded with rubies as big as hen's eggs, to satisfy half a zoo. Now, having licked her chops, cheeks, chin, and paws clean, she was guzzling away at a goblet of red wine, which she held clumsily but daintily enough in both forepaws.

Grrff eyed her surreptitiously. No more than a week before, when he and Ganelon and a little boy named Phadia had strayed into the hyperspatial labyrinth, gotten lost, and ended up in a magical place called the Halfworld, he had been conducting a yowling flirtation with a lady sphinx who had just gone into heat. They had left the Halfworld just a bit too soon, from his way of thinking. Now he kept eyeing the huge breasts of Ishgadara speculatively.*

From time to time the Gynosphinx met his sly gaze with a full stare from her own enormous, round, emerald-green orbs.

---

*These events may be found in Chapters 18-21 of *The Enchantress of World's End*, the Second Book of the Gondwane Epic. The sphinxes of the Halfworld are genuinely mythological beasts, fully capable of breeding, unlike the quasi-sphinxes of Gondwane.

She grinned at him demurely, twitching her cat-whiskers quite fetchingly, and once she tipped him a deliberate wink. Grrff felt nonplussed, and was entertaining some notions of finding out on his own whether Gynosphinxes were truly lacking in the organs of gender.

For quite some time now Palensus Choy and his fat friend, Ollub Vetch, had been explaining their mission, its purpose and cause, to bewildered old Yemple, who smiled placidly, went tut-tut frequently, and hardly understood a word of what was being said. From time to time the jovial monarch picked up a corner of the tablecloth to swab his dripping brow. Entertaining powerful magicians, who could turn you into a yerxel or a Youk as easy as pie, he found a trifle disconcerting. Still, this was the sort of thing kings did all the time, he supposed.

After lunch, Princess Slioma danced for them. She was a slim, black-eyed gypsy girl, with innumerable scarlet petticoats, a vivacious and dazzling smile, and a prematurely lush pair of bosoms which threatened to pop out of her low-cut gown at any moment. Palensus Choy blinked amiably, if sleepily, at the view, but Ollub Vetch—who fancied himself as something of a ladies' man—ogled the voluptuous teen-aged charmer with intent interest.

They went for a stroll on the tier of the Royal Ziggurat, the two savants, Ganelon, Xarda the girl knight, and Prince Erigon, who was eager to find out how Valardus was managing to defend itself. Grrff volunteered to entertain the huge lady sphinx, who smiled demurely and padded along at his side with a rolling gait, because of the immense breadth of her chest, which had to be inordinately broad not only so that her shoulder muscles might be sufficiently developed to drive her mighty wings, but also so as to accommodate her enormous breasts.

After a little desultory conversation, the Tigerman found Ishgadara to be much more intelligent and articulate than his former lady-love whom he had left behind, however unwillingly, in the Halfworld. She had a deep, hoarse voice whose timbre was that of a buzzsaw cutting through a tough oak tree, and an inability to pronounce the letters 'b' or 'v' (because of the shortness of her upper lip), which lent to her speech a slight trace of a lisp he found delightful. In person, and close up, she exuded a strong musky smell, like an immense unwashed dog, which was not entirely unpleasant, mixed with a sweetish, milky sort of odor. Her size, though, he found intimidating. Her forelimbs were as big around at the wrist as his legs were at the thighs, and her paws were as big as his own head. She could have splattered his brains across the deck of the tier with a playful swat, he knew, and this was nervous-making.

It was hard to feel amorous toward something that could brain you with a slap. The females of his race, if less bosomy, were at least smaller than he, and docile.

Still, he discovered that he liked her, and found her rough-and-ready sense of humor enjoyable. They soon became fast friends, once the possibilities of an amorous encounter were clearly out of the question.

"Tell me, lass," he rumbled with affectionate jocularity, "how long have you been with this Palensus Choy fellow?"

"Not long," she purred throatily. "Pefore long, will be maype six month. He make me, you know, cat-man."

"Made you? How did he make you?" he inquired curiously.

She gave a humorous shrug, and rolled her great green moony eyes.

"Ishgadara no knowingk that! Too youngk at the time. Skinny master have preedingk vats, lotsa preedingk vats. Make many of myth-a-logick monsters. He collect um."

"But none so fetching as you, my lass, I'll wager," the Tigerman chuckled, nudging the lady sphinx in the ribs.

She nudged back, nearly knocking him flat. Scrambling up with a hasty laugh, trying to ignore the pang of bruised ribs, he resolved on no more nudging, unless he was wearing some of Xarda's armor.

"Breeding vats, eh? That's interesting. Tell me about his palace, won't you?"

"Sure!" she rumbled agreeably. "Pig place, lotsa rooms in um. Ishgadara got whole stall all ta herself. Fat li'l master, he come six-seffen months ago. Alla time they fight offer magic er science. Make Ishgadara laughink, when they fight."

Then, with a shrewd sideways glance, she asked purringly: "You no man-sphinx like Ishgadara, right?"

"No, m'lass, I'm what they call a Tigerman. But your master made me too, in a way. At least, he made my ancestors. Didn't know he was still alive, Palensus Choy . . . . but why do you ask?"

She managed to look sly and coy at the same time.

"Ishgadara neffer meet no man-sphinx pefore, not effen no Tigerman like you. Neffer see no sphinx cups, either."

" 'Sphinx cups'?" he repeated, puzzled. "Oh, I get you, Ish-gadara: sphinx *cubs.*"

"Sure! You know, papies."

"Yes, babies. If what your master says is true, and you have no gender, and no, ah, sex, then I guess there couldn't *be* any baby sphinxes," he said.

She rolled her eyes comically, and swung her shoulders so that her huge, splendid mammaries swung to and fro like great fat pinkish bells. "Then what *these* for?" she asked.

He swallowed, grinned feebly, and changed the subject as fast as possible.

"The siege of Valardus is now at a stalemate," the lanky long-bearded old magician was saying at that precise moment, in reply to a question from Prince Erigon.

"How can that be?" demanded the Prince reasonably. "When I left Valardus, it was in momentary threat of invasion, and what with our lack of troops or trained fighting men of any kind, my royal father's realm couldn't have held off the Barbarians for half an afternoon, much less all these weeks!"

"The wall of fire somewhat dampens the enthusiasm of the ruffians, of course," murmured Palensus Choy offhandedly.

"*What* wall of fire?" cried Erigon in exasperation. It was hard for the polite young man to lose his temper, but trying to get information out of the vague and rather absent-minded magician was enough to try the patience of a godling.

"From the oil wells, you know. To the north of the city."

Erigon nodded; a source of the rare fossil fuel had been discovered in the hills beyond the city before his birth, and afforded the Valardines an excellent source of revenue. Although machinery of any sophistication was seldom used in Gondwane in this Eon, the black petroleum served excellently as a lubricant for cartwheels or chariots, and for oil lamps.

"Go on."

"Your father's Court Philosopher, I believe it was, suggested digging a moat entirely around the city proper, directing the pipeline therein, and touching fire to the gooey stuff. It burns splendidly, and the supply seems inexhaustible. The only trouble I foresee will be, ahem, finding a way to extinguish the blaze once the Ximchak ruffians have wandered off to destroy some other place."

Prince Erigon looked dazed. He had more than half expected to find Valardus a heap of smoldering rubble by this time. Instead, the unwarlike Valardines had somehow managed to hold the Horde at bay—incredible!

"Old Ningovus thought that one up?" he murmured. "I can hardly believe it!"

"My boy, you can see it for yourself," said Palensus Choy pleasantly. "At our current rate of travel, we should be there by tomorrow morning."

4.

The Ximchaks Are Routed

Since the aerial invasion had not, after all, turned out to be an aerial invasion, the inhabitants of Kan Zar Kan enjoyed the fireworks display and street picnic which had originally been scheduled for that evening.

The former Iomagoths, and their honored guests and visitors, went to their beds replete and happy. Darkness fell; the immense, swollen bulk of Old Earth's ancient companion, the Moon, heaved up her cracked but still-radiant face over the horizon, turning the night into a dim silvery almost-day. The Mobile City continued due north across the leagues of whispering grass, its running lights blinking scarlet and green, searchlights sweeping the prairie before it to ascertain if any dangerous obstacles blocked its way. None did.

The Falling Moon, which had come far closer to Earth than in our time, and was nearly at Roche's Limit by this Eon, floated up the sky and gradually declined down the other side of the heavens. Morning came, in the form of a pallid and ghostly luminance, redly gold. Then the Sun rose and it was day.

By daylight the Kan Zar Kanians perceived that the horizon to the north was crowned by an immense rampart of mountains which marched across Gondwane the Great from east to west. As the light sharpened and grew brighter, the dim blue cloudiness of this rampart drew into focus, as it were, separating into individual peaks.

Sometime just before dawn, Kan Zar Kan had crossed the invisible boundary which divided Northern YamaYamaLand from Greater Zuavia. That colossal wall of soaring peaks was none other than the Carthazian Mountains, a titanic chain that could have formed the backbone of a continent, and once had.

Prince Erigon directed the City to cruise along below the rampart until he could recognize a landmark. Soon one appeared, and he instructed the City to continue in its present direction for another hour, at which time they would reach the site of his father's Kingdom of Valardus.

They saw the smoke of the fiery moat around the city long before it was possible to identify the actual spires of Valardus. A towering plume of oily black vapors ascended in the clear morning light, gradually inclining before a brisk breeze to the east, as swift winds shredded its upper works into long streamers of smoke.

Approaching, the City slowed to a halt, fan rotors idling, while Ganelon Silvermane and his companions, together with the immortal magician Palensus Choy and the fat inventor, Ollub Vetch, climbed to the observation deck atop the central ziggurat, to observe the lay of the land through powerful optical instruments.

They rejoiced to discover that the Ximchak warriors as yet had not succeeded in taking Valardus, for the flaming moat remained unbridged and the city walls bore a full garrison in the purple-and-silver livery of the Valardine Monarchy. But the savages of the Horde lay encamped in a vast semicircle before the besieged city, and seemed very numerous. Orniths, as the beaked and feathered steeds of the Gondwanians in this age were called, were penned in rude corrals. Red felt tents grew like mushrooms after a rainstorm along the hills and slopes of the Carthazians. From the numerousness of these tents, Ganelon and Grrff estimated the strength of the besieging army to be about five thousand fighting men.

At this place there was a huge notch cut into the mountainous wall, about thirty square miles in extent, which had formerly been the fertile valley farmland surrounding the city. The farms were long since laid waste, the fields trampled into dust, the cattle butchered to feed the Ximchaks.

At the far or northern end of the valley of Valardus, a great gap could be seen in the mountains. This was the famous Luzar Pass by which the Barbarians had crossed the Carthazian Mountains from the country of the Gomps.

It was obvious that only a minor portion of the great Horde had come down through the mountains to lay siege to

Valardus. Therefore, the majority of the savage Barbarians must still be investing the Thirty Cities of the Gompish Regime, which they had reputedly invaded and crushed a year or so earlier, descending out of the north.

"Five thousand isn't so very many," mused Ganelon thoughtfully. "But it's more than we could fight." Slioma, the teen-aged Iomagothic Princess, vigorously disagreed.

"We 'uns c'n take um," she argued. "Ol' City, here, 'll fightum. You hear, City?"

"Yes, Princess," replied the voder-voice of the City Brain in its calm, synthetic baritone. "But let your City point out that while the valley itself is flat enough to negotiate on the air-cushion drive, the width of the Luzar Pass is not sufficient for your City to enter, much less to traverse."

"Sojers—a-comin'!" chirped Kurdi excitedly. The bright-eyed little page gestured wildly, calling to their attention the fact that a sizable detachment of Ximchaks had left the main camp and were riding out onto the Purple Plains in order to investigate the unknown city of glittering metal which had so mysteriously appeared in view.

"Those aren't soldiers, Kurdi; they are Barbarians," observed Ganelon. He and Grrff had taken a liking to the clever, vivacious little gypsy boy, and had been teaching him how to use a sword. Unlike the rest of the Iomagoths, who were generally a shiftless lot, he seemed to show some promise of being made of keener stuff. The orphan had been adopted as King Yemple's official page at their suggestion.

"What's th' diff'rince?" inquired Kurdi impatiently.

"Soldiers are disciplined, and fight in orderly formations," Silvermane explained. "Barbarians fight as an unruly mob, and can easily be stampeded into panicky flight. Or so I hope, anyway," the bronze giant added to himself.

"The riders are approaching the perimeter of your City," announced the City placidly. "Shall I take evasive action, or attack?"

"A good question," growled Grrff, hefting his long-handled ygdraxel uneasily. "Big man, these Iomagoths won't stand and fight, so it's up to us—"

"The war party has just reached my edge and is riding along it while arguing as to whether to board me or not," Kan Zar Kan reported in a pleasantly neutral voice. "Shall I activate my air cushion, reverse the suction, and draw the warriors into my rotor blades, using the strategem which proved excellently successful when I was attacked by the Death Dwarves from the Kingdom of Red Magic?"*

Ganelon debated within himself, then shook his head, tousling his waist-length glittering mane.

"No; that's our secret weapon. Let's save it until the Ximchaks attack us in force. Has King Yemple stationed the Royal Archers on the rooftops along Avenue J, as I suggested?"

"He has," replied the City Brain, "but less than half of them have reported for duty."

"Where are the rest of 'em?" growled Grrff belligerently.

"On sick call, suffering from a variety of complaints which range from toothache, earache, and upset stomach to ingrown toenails, hemorrhoids, and acid indigestion."

"Hmph," snorted Xarda. "By my troth, such malingerers would be drummed out of the Nine Knightly Orders for such scandalous and cowardly behavior—in Jemmerdy, of course."

"Of course," grumbled Grrff. "And ol' Grrff wishes they *were* in Jemmerdy! What d'you think, big man, can we take 'em with the few we got?"

"I guess we'll have to," shrugged Ganelon, a trifle grimly. "Few as they are, at least they're armed with those hollow arrowheads stuffed with impact-sensitive explosive powder the City made up for us. A lucky thing the Memory Tanks contained a complete knowledge of chemistry. City, would you please give the signal to the archers to commence firing."

"With pleasure," replied Kan Zar Kan. Moments later there came the sound of dull explosions from the edge of the dish-shaped mobile metropolis. Plumes of smoke ascended the air.

"Who's got the hand bombs?" inquired Silvermane.

"Right here," said Grrff, slapping—gently—the fat and bulging knapsack he wore slung over one furry shoulder.

"Take the flying kayak and—"

"Flyingk kayak, pool!" snorted a hoarse voice behind them. "Takingk *me!*"

Ganelon turned, saw Ishgadara poised atop the crest of the Red Ziggurat, caught an indignant glare from her moony eyes, grinned sheepishly, and nodded his assent.

"Then it's you and Grrff, my lass," growled the Tigerman

---

*The City refers to a scene described in the Second Book of the Epic, *The Enchantress of World's End*. See in particular Chapters 26-27.

happily, climbing between her huge shoulders and grabbing a
fistful of her lionlike mane between his fingers. She grinned,
opened her great bronze-feathered wings with an audible
snap, like a giant's fan. A moment later she leaped into the
air, wings drumming, and rose in a wobbling curve, circled
the city's disc, and dove down toward its distant edge. They
saw Grrff dig one paw into his sack and hurl something down-
ward. A few black arrows came lofting up toward him, but
fell short. Then a muffled boom sounded, and a cloud of
angry whirling smoke rose into view. The arrows stopped.
More booms followed.

"Shall I help our worthy comrade?" inquired Prince Erigon. "I can take the flying kayak—"

"*We* will take the flying kayak," insisted Xarda.

"Thanks, but it only takes one to throw the hand bombs."

"Quite so," the girl knight nodded crisply. "But I need you
to work the foot pedals. Come along! Ganelon, we do have
have more of those little bombs, don't we?"

"Right over there; Kurdi's been guarding them," Silvermane grinned.

A few moments later the ungainly length of Istrobian's
flying kayak came into view, angling around the dome atop
the Red Ziggurat. Prince Erigon was pumping the pedals up
and down while Xarda was unlimbering the bomblets.

Soon a double chorus of booms came from the edge of
Kan Zar Kan. The Ximchaks broke into disorder, and went
galloping on their fear-maddened bird-horses in every direction. Fighting against a Moving City was all very well, but
being attacked from the air by half-human tigers riding on
flying lions—to say nothing of lady knights in flying contrap-
tions—was something new to the poor Barbarians, and they
did not enjoy the novelty.

The first battle of Kan Zar Kan ended about ten minutes
later in a complete rout.

5.

Making Mincemeat of the Enemy

The victory luncheon was held in the Central Square, a newly built plaza situated before the Grand Entrance to the Red Ziggurat, or Royal Palace, as it was now known. Medals were hastily struck by the City, which retooled one bench of the machine shop for that purpose, in gold, platinum, silver, iridium, and *queasium.**

King Yemple passed out the new medals—Royal Order of the Defenders of Kan Zar Kan, First, Second, Third, and Fourth Class—with a liberal hand. Erigon, Xarda, Ishgadara, and Grrff got them as a matter of course, but so did those of the Royal Archers who were lucky enough not to have been suffering from the afflictions of earache, toothache, etc., when the chips were down. Grrff got one struck in *queasium;* by the third course of the Victory Luncheon he developed an attack of hiccoughs, and before they subsided the comcomitant vibrations had jarred the *queasium* through half the precious metals known to metallurgy.

King Yemple so heartily enjoyed handing out his new medals (*and* drinking a toast to each individual so honored) that he had to be forcibly restrained from pinning one on the flying kayak.

By early afternoon, a major detachment rode out from the Ximchak camp. The City estimated their numbers to be in the vicinity of six hundred mounted warriors.

*A synthetic metal, so named from its extreme instability. So unstable is *queasium* that, at any moment, it transmutes itself into diamond, ruby, emerald, or wuthunx-crystals. For those who like to know such details, the element *queasium* is Number 118 on the Periodic Table, with an atomic weight of 269.

"Not enough," grunted Ganelon. "Take evasive action."

All afternoon the Mobile City glided back and forth on its hissing air cushion, dodging with ease the exasperated Ximchaks, now numbering over one thousand. They shook their fists at the elusive metropolis, and yelled curses after it, demanding it stand its ground and fight like a man.

Toward early evening the unequal race between Kan Zar Kan and Ximchaks had drawn so much interest and attention from the besieging Horde that over two thousand of the Barbarian warriors were engaged in chasing it back and forth.

"That's enough, I guess," Ganelon decided. "We can't keep this up forever."

At his order, the City now turned about and slowed to a halt and sat there with engines idling. Yelling triumphantly, the Ximchaks closed in from all sides. They were chocolate-brown of skin, their bushy beards teased into fat ringlets, miniature gold statuettes representing their savage pantheon dangling like earrings from pierced lobes.

Through some genetic oddity the irises of their eyes were of a brilliant scarlet, which they emphasized by painting green circles around their eyes. Their leather helmets were horned with Youk-antlers; they wore heavy-lacquered leather tunics with short flat-skirts, in back and in front, and slit up the sides. Their brown legs were bound in criss-cross gaiters made of supple leather thongs about two inches wide, looking for all the world like mummy wrappings.

They were bowlegged, broad-shouldered, long-armed, bloodthirsty, and wild with war-fury after a dusty and exhausting afternoon of chasing the elusive City back and forth. Massed in denser ranks, for once, they charged the City at full tilt, waving their weapons and yelling themselves hoarse.

"Now!" said Ganelon.

The City changed its gears—a sound like someone clearing his throat—and reversed the suction of the air cushion upon which it rode. The suction was terrific. Like a colossal vacuum cleaner it sucked full-grown warriors into the whirring fan blades underneath the dish-shaped structure upon which Kan Zar Kan was built. Yelling with astonishment, the warriors slid into the fan blades. So did most of their unhappy orniths, as well, for the miniature hurricane generated by the powerful fans did not discriminate between ornith and rider.

A few moments later, the City changed gears again, and

reversed the suction to normal. Vents opened in the flanks of the metal metropolis. A pinkish-brown and rather watery stew sprayed the surrounding meadows—all that remained of several hundred Ximchak warriors after they had passed through the whirring fan blades.

The remainder of the warriors who had pursued the elusive City across the prairie stopped short, goggle-eyed, struck speechless. Those nearest to the City became soaked to the skin with the greasy stew of minced Ximchak and ornith which squirted from the vents.

"Now give 'em a taste of their own medicine!" roared Grrff delightedly.

Obediently, the City got under way again. Only this time it no longer fled from the pursuing Ximchaks—it charged down upon them! They broke in dismay, fleeing in all directions. But there were quite a few of them who did not flee quite fast enough and were sucked into the fans when next the direction of the blowers was reversed. As soon as their remains had served to fertilize the purple grasses of the Plain, the City went trundling off toward the largest party in flight, gobbling them up, too.

By that time, the rest had made a speedy return to the tents of their brethren, jumped down, and explained what had occurred to their bewildered fellows with much waving of arms and loud curses.

Whether or not the more stay-at-home-minded of the Ximchaks quite understood what had befallen remains an unanswered question. A moot point, you might say. Also an unimportant detail—for soon it became obvious that the murderous metropolis was headed straight for the main camp.

Ximchaks came boiling out of their tents like a swarm of maddened bees. The City hurtled toward them, came to a sharp stop, and abruptly reversed its engines yet again. Warriors, orniths, tents, and everything else that wasn't tied down got pulled into the fans.

Watching a full hundred and fifty of the enemy vanish beneath the edge of the City in a single gulp, Prince Erigon chuckled delightedly.

"Now, this is what *I* call a civilized way to fight a war!" he smiled. He was seated languidly on the parapet of the palace, nibbling on a leg of roast prairie fowl, his appetite none the worse for observing the pinkish soup, which had been a hundred and fifty Barbarians a moment before, go spraying in all directions.

"No doubt," sniffed Xarda. " 'Tis against every rule of chivalry, of course—but what would the likes of *you* know about *that!*"

"Very little, I'm afraid," smiled the Prince, obviously unoffended. "I am interested in winning wars, not in fighting them by some set of arbitrary and unrealistic rules."

The glint of battle showed in Xarda's eye and in the way she gritted her teeth. Sensing they were about to be given a shrill-voiced lecture in Fundamental Chivalry, Palensus Choy tactfully interrupted.

"My dear young lady, surely the important thing is to relieve Valardus before it is destroyed by these savages," he murmured politely. "And how we accomplish it is of far less importance than is the fact that we do, after all, accomplish it. Am I not correct? Would you not share the emotions of Prince Erigon, if, for example, it were Jemmerdy and not Valardus we were defending at this moment?"

Xarda choked off a terse retort, looking grim and mutinous, then thoughtful. She subsided with a lame apology, which the amiable young Prince accepted gracefully.

Pausing from time to time to gobble up a few hundred more Ximchaks, Kan Zar Kan slowly drew a half-circle about Valardus, just outside of the wall of fire. As it passed, not only did the Ximchaks vanish, but so did all signs of their occupancy of these farms and fields—tents, earthworks, ornith corrals, cookfires, everything. Even the latrines.

By late afternoon, the City had made mincemeat out of as many of the former members of the besieging host as it could catch, and the siege was over.

The survivors had taken to their heels, and the smarter of them had also taken to the hills. Since the one thing the Mobile City could not do was to climb a hill, it was left to Ganelon and Grrff, astride Ishgadara, and Xarda, Erigon and the little boy, Kurdi, aboard Istrobian's flying kayak, to dispose of them.

Remaining well out of reach of the Ximchak arrows, the flying kayak and the Gynosphinx tracked the fleeing Ximchaks and blew them into fragments with the hand bombs, until by early twilight they had exhausted the supply of explosives—and also the supply of live Ximchaks.

They flew back to Kan Zar Kan in time for supper, weary,

wind-burnt, smoke-blackened, with aching arms, but with a sense of mission accomplished.

King Yemple greeted them on the landing tier of the Royal Palace with open arms.

"If he tries to pin another medal on Grrff this time, Grrff'll give him a fat lip to go with the rest o' him!" growled the weary, smoke-dirty Karjixian.

"Why do you say that?" asked Ganelon.

Grrff pointed a thumb at his furry chest.

Jolted about by the afternoon's flying, the *queasium* medal had run the gamut of crystalline substances, given up the ghost, and turned itself into dull lead. And there it stayed— the only Order of the Defenders of Kan Zar Kan, *Fifth* Class, ever struck.

Laughing, the bomb throwers dismounted and went into the palace for a hot bath, or a hot supper, or, quite likely, both.

For a time, at least, the war was over.

Or the first skirmish, anyway.

6.

A Royal Welcome in Valardus

That very evening about sundown, they entered into Valardus. While the Mobile City of Kan Zar Kan stood guard against any further incursion on the part of the wrathful Ximchaks, by parking in the mouth of the Luzar Pass, thus effectively blocking the way, Ganelon and his friends entered into the city of Good King Vergus.

The wall of fire, now happily no longer needed, was extinguished through a minor thaumaturgy cast by Palensus Choy. The absent-minded magician, well versed in the Sixty Sciences after innumerable millennia of study, employed a variety of Elemental Magic, called the Undinic, or Sea Magic, for this purpose. The Elemental of Water effectively put out the raging flames, leaving a residue of thick black sludgelike oil trickling along the bottom of the fire-blackened ditch which could easily be set afire again, should the Ximchaks, or any other enemy, appear later on.

The Undine herself was not visible, merely a damp greenish cloud which settled upon the blazing moat, which dwindled and died at her touch.

Ollub Vetch sniffed in disdain and refused to witness this use of the occult forces he despised.

"Hoy!" he snorted. "And couldn't I do as well with me physical sciences, with just a bit o' time at me disposal? A little dabblin' with me chemistry, and I c'd find a counteragent to smother them flames. But—oh, no! His high-and-mighty magicianship, over there, he has to use his silly spells an' cantrips!"

"Nemmind," giggled the gypsy boy, Kurdi, soothingly, "maybe they let you do some chemistry later on."

The Valardines turned out in force to welcome their saviors. Prince Erigon, in his least threadbare tabard and wearing for this formal occasion his princely coronet, entered the city first, with Ganelon Silvermane and Grrff the Xombolian, in Istrobian's flying kayak.

Xarda, her armor burnished to a mirrory gleam, rode beside King Yemple and Kurdi, his page, in a chariot whipped up for the event in the Kan Zar Kanian machine shops, which was drawn by a team of mournful-looking and slightly windblown Ximchak orniths, which had escaped the general destruction.

Palensus Choy and his fat inventor friend followed at a discreet distance, mounted on Ishgadara the Gynosphinx, whose mane and tail were braided into innumerable pigtails, each tied with a ribbon of silver or purple, the Royal Valardine Colors.

The Valardine populace lined the broad avenues to welcome them, and crowded the rooftops and the balconies which overlooked the triumphal procession as it wended its way through the city to the King's castle, which rose on a height at the center of the pleasant little city.

Xarda peered about interestedly. Valardus was gay and colorful, with houses of creamy stucco, roofed with red tiles, and squat domes of mellow brick topped with green bronze spires, from which fluttered silver-and-purple bannerols charged with the royal heraldry. The people cheered them loudly, waving little flags, and those on the rooftops dropped small bouquets of flowers upon them as they went by.

Good King Vergus met them on the steps of the castle, together with the assembled peers and nobility of the realm. There were an immense throng of these, some in heraldic tabards and others in robes of estates, some bearing ceremonial batons or maces, others in an enormous variety of crowns, coronets, circlets, and ermine-trimmed and gold-betassled chapeaux of red or blue or gold or purple velvet. Many had retainers who stood near, bearing up rich-colored flags, banners and bannerols, ensigns and standards denoting their presence.

It was quite a crowd, and they were introduced to so many notables that it soon became impossible for any of the visitors to remember which was an Earl, a Count, or a Baron, or to tell the Dukes from the Grand Dukes or the Archdukes. Grrff, rather in bewilderment, grumbled to Xarda that it looked to *him* as if the aristocracy of Valardus outnumbered

the commoners three to one. Prince Erigon, nearby, over-
heard this remark and smilingly said that this was, in fact,
the case.

"Valardus is a quaint, cozy, old-fashioned sort of kingdom," he explained, "with a long and glorious history filled
with remarkable achievements and illustrious deeds. To com-
memorate each of these, the monarchs of my Royal Father's
line have raised to the peerage, or ennobled, virtually every
family in the realm at one time or another."

"*What* illustrious deeds?" inquired Xarda. "I understood
that Valardus had no martial history to speak of, and that its
annals were remarkably free of wars, conquests, or invasions."

"Quite so," the Prince murmured, with a faint smile. "In a
realm so peace-loving as Valardus, quite another kind of
deed is regarded as worthy of a peerage." Indicating a tall,
solemn personage in a gorgeously emblazoned tabard, just
then being introduced to Ganelon Silvermane, Erigon said:
"The Archduke Fazlark, there, for example. His thirteenth
grandsire introduced the first masquerade ball to Valardus,
and was ennobled for this sterling deed."

"What does the Archduke do now?"

"He is my father's gardener."

"Oh."

In swift succession they met a Marchioness whose ances-
tor had invented a new kind of fireworks display; she was the
upstairs maid. And a Viscount, who doubled as a boot-
black, and whose remotest forefather had innovated a
novel card game. To say nothing of a Baronet who was a
streetcleaner, and whose great-grandfather had achieved the
lesser nobility through a delightful propensity for inventing
crossword puzzles.

As for King Vergus himself, he turned out to be a remarkably short, remarkably stout, remarkably red-faced
little man, beaming with smiles, bald as a tomato except for
fugituve wisps of snowy hair curling about his ears. He resembled, therefore, both King Yemple and Ollub Vetch.

He came waddling down the steps from the landing where
the Grand Dukes, Archdukes, and common or everyday
Dukes were standing, beaming expansively and puffing with
pride.

"My boy, my boy!" he wheezed, throwing his arms around
the neck of his son (well, around his waist, actually, since
he was too short to reach that high up on the Prince). "A

joyous day of triumph and victory for Valardus! You certainly accomplished your mission in the grand manner, although it took you long enough to get back with some reinforcements! You must tell me the whole story, begob!"

"Later, sire. First I want you to meet my friend—*our* friends, actually—the true saviors of Valardus. This is his majesty King Yemple of Kan Zar Kan, and Ganelon Silvermane, the Hero of Uth, who whelmed the Indigons last year, and this is his friend Grrff the Xombolian, a war chieftain of Karjixia, and the Sirix Xarda of Jemmerdy, one of those lady knights they have down there, and, ah, let me see, oh, yes, this is the celebrated Immortal of Zaradon, Palensus Choy, and his colleague, the famous inventor and scientist Ollub Vetch, and Kurdi, of course, that's King Yemple's page, and Ishgadara, a Gynosphinx, one of Palensus Choy's animals. Hm . . . yes, I think that's all."

King Vergus was a trifle overwhelmed, but he was happy to welcome them all in the name of Valardus, even if he did persist in mixing up all of their names. For the longest time thereafter he insisted on calling Ganelon "Gynosphinx" and Xarda "Xombolian," and the two visiting savants "Palensus Vetch" and "Ollub Choy," much to their annoyance.

Indeed, I'm not entirely certain that he ever *did* get all of their names sorted out properly; not, of course, that it really mattered.

Once they had met all of the peers, the King led them into the Grand Hall of the castle, where another company awaited them. These, it seemed, were the really important courtiers and officers of the realm, although they were only knights-bachelor. Sir Azrak, a lean, dour individual with a tuft of iron-colored beard, turned out to be the Chamberlain, and a gracious, smiling, innocuous-looking man of medium height called Sir Belery was the Marshal. An aged duffer, very hard of hearing, named Sir Cardoy, was the Lord Treasurer, while they were given to understand the mousy little man in the corner, who hardly said a word, was Sir Lamoral, the Secretary of State, Lord Privy Councilor, and Hereditary First Minister of the Crown.

These important men wore threadbare tunics, patched tights, and ragged cloaks, in striking contrast to the host of gorgeously robed greengrocers, farmers, blacksmiths, and garbage collectors they had met on the front steps. Ganelon asked why.

"Quite simple, young sir," puffed the King good-humoredly. "In a realm chock full of Grandees and Arch-Ducal Highnesses, the only way to stand out from the throng is to be a simple landless knight. Have some tea, everyone!"

Incidentally, before the evening was done he had knighted them all.

7.

The Victory Feast

Dinner that evening was held in the Grand Hall, and the high officers of state were all invited. They seemed happy to be offered a good meal, and fell to as if famished.

Xarda, who was seated next to the tall, sour-faced Chamberlain, Sir Azrak, told of their most recent adventures, but was unable to make herself heard over the gaunt old knight's slurping-up of his soup. She soon lapsed into grim silence.

Prince Erigon, seated at his father's left, right next to quiet little Sir Belery, the Lord Marshal of the Realm, explained—over Sir Belery's munching of a crisp salad, of which he downed four servings—how his wanderings in search of mercenaries had led him south to Chx, and into jail there, where he had fortunately made the acquaintance of his new friends.

King Vergus was fascinated by the whole account, and begged further details about the amazing Mobile City from its pudgy monarch, the ex-gypsy chief, King Yemple. Yemple, more than a bit nervous at his first exposure to genuine royalty, soon relaxed and began to enjoy himself, although from time to time he could not help slipping a few of the soupspoons into his voluminous belt-pouch. They were solid gold, after all, and old habits die hard.

Grrff's sly eyes noticed this, but the Tigerman said nothing. Let King Vergus guard his own soup spoons!

Sir Cardoy, the old Lord Treasurer, munched toothlessly on everything that was set before him, paying no attention to the conversation which went on around him. This was not rudeness on the old man's part, as he was simply oblivious to most of what was being said. When you are hard of hearing, you can seem rude without giving offense.

Palensus Choy dealt manfully with the festive board, but did not seem particularly hungry. He chewed and swallowed with such a curious expression of interest, rather than hunger, that finally Ganelon asked him about it. The absent-minded magician smiled dreamily.

"But my dear boy, I haven't eaten anything but a bit of salad, a ripe fruit, or a glass of the convivial grape in tens of thousands of years, and I do so now only for the sake of politeness! To be an immortal, in the sense of the word in which I am one, is to be invulnerable to destruction. This, of course, includes starvation as well as injury or sickness or age. Thus I have long since gotten out of the habit of imbibing sustenance from need, and do so now only out of politeness."

Ganelon was looking a trifle dubious, remembering earlier in Kan Zar Kan how inexhaustible a trencherman Choy had appeared when King Yemple served them lunch. Glancing up, he caught a merry wink from Ollub Vetch.

"Pay no attention to himself, there," whispered the fat inventor. "He eats enough fer two men. It be his vanity to pertend to abstain from anything so grossly common as food!"

Ganelon nodded, faintly smiling. Choy was still crunching away, and hadn't heard this exchange.

"Yes, my boy," he continued, downing a pint of wine at a gulp, "we immortals simply never eat. My body, you see, sustains itself by absorption of the zeta-theta-beta radiation given off by Old Earth's palindromic energy field. Were this not so, I would be vulnerable to destruction through starvation, hence no true immortal at all, merely (ahem!) a very long-lived old gentleman. Hmm . . . what do they call these tasty gobbets, I wonder?"

"Roast zooky-zooky bird gizzards," said Ollub Vetch cheerfully. "Dipped in tree-turnip sauce. Delicious, aren't they?"

"Sorry I asked," said Choy disapprovingly. "I happen to be exceedingly fond of zooky-zooky birds."

"So am *I*" beamed Ollub Vetch with a gleam in his eye, shoveling another large helping of the roast gizzards onto his plate.

These plates, incidentally, were also of solid gold, but somewhat too large to have fitted into even the capacious pouch of King Yemple. That worthy monarch eyed them unhappily from time to time during the meal, but could not think of a way to purloin a few.

Sir Lamoral, the colorless, timid little Secretary of State, finishing his repast, wiped his lips daintily and settled back in his chair, cradling between his hands a huge goblet brim full of red wine. The cup was the size of Sir Lamoral's head, which was rather small, but the little man guzzled away at it thirstily, and soon asked in a polite whisper for a refill.

Prince Erigon, having concluded an account of his own wanderings and adventures with Ganelon Silvermane and Grrff the Xombolian and the Sirix Xarda, turned the conversation back to Valardus. Confessing himself amazed to have discovered that the beleaguered city had for such a lengthy time managed to escape destruction at the hands of the Ximchak Barbarians, the affable young Prince inquired after the full story. Beaming fondly, his father the King complied.

"Well, m'boy, as ye know, we 'ad expected the filthy savages to come down on us in full strength, but, as things turned out, begob, only a teensy-tiny portion of they great ugly brutes came through the Pass, the ugly hairy beasts, to lay they siege of our brave city—"

"About one-fortieth of the whole, sire," mumbled Sir Ningovus, the Court Philosopher.

"One-fortieth!" repeated Prince Erigon, blankly. He stared off into space for a few moments, his lips moving soundlessly. Then he jumped, paled, and looked stricken.

"You mean, sire, there are still *nearly two hundred thousand* of the Barbarians beyond the mountain-barrier?"

"Eh?" murmured the King. "Well, hah, whatever . . . back in Gompish territory, m'boy . . . minus however many thousands that wonderful murderin' city of yours chopped into beef stew."

"But we only killed about three thousand of the five thousand or so Barbarian warriors in the siege camp," protested Prince Erigon.

"Five thousand six hundred and forty-three," mumbled Sir Ningovus, the Court Philosopher. He was a medium-sized, middle-aged, average-looking, rather nondescript little man in threadbare robes, with a smudge of oil on one cheek and a distracted air. Throughout the meal he had been conversing animatedly with Ollub Vetch, the fat inventor. It seemed that Sir Ningovus was by hobby a machinist, by talent an inventor, and by profession a philosopher—of natural philosophy, that is, which is to say, a sort of scientist. He was fascinated to meet the celebrated Vetch, one of his idols, and

the two had talked a mile a minute through the length of
the nineteen-course banquet, mostly about perpetual motion.

King Vergus blinked blankly.

"Oh, ah," he said feebly. "Is that all you killed? Me goodness, but—"

The Valardines present looked at one another in growing
consternation. It had not really yet come home to them, in
the mood of euphoric victory which had followed the lifting
of the siege, how precarious their position still remained.

True, one-fortieth of the Ximchak Horde had been either
slaughtered or driven into ignominious flight.

But what about the other thirty-nine fortieths?

"Zaar will never swallow such a setback," groaned Sir
Azrak in sepulchral tones. "The villainous dastard will descend upon our fair realm Valardine in all his force, to grind
us into the dust!"

"Zaar? Who is Zaar?" inquired Ollub Vetch anxiously.

"The Warlord of the Ximchak Barbarians," said Ganelon
heavily. "My master, the Illusionist, used to call him one of
the three most potentially dangerous forces threatening the
peace and security of these parts of Gondwane. A war leader of brilliance and even genius; he is ambitious, and very
dangerous."

"All dangerous men are ambitious," said Palensus Choy,
with the solemn tones one uses when quoting a weighty
maxim. The others regarded him a bit askance, since in this
case his maxim did not seem to make any particular sense.
He flushed, and grinned feebly.

"Ahem! All *ambitious* men are *dangerous,* that is," he
amended himself hastily, with a little laugh. "Heh, this wine,
you know, really goes to one's head and stirs one's wits about
terribly! Especially if you haven't drunk more than half a
cup in half a thousand years . . ."

"Hrrmph. Hah. Yes. Well," said Good King Vergus nervously. "Perchance the good fella will just stay up north,
there, grindin' the pore old Gomps into th' dust, and leave us
be."

"Perchance," intoned Sir Azrak gloomily.

There ensued a considerable interval of silence, broken
only by the munching and crunching of little Sir Belery,
still at work among the celery, to say nothing of the radishes.

"Well," said Grrff uncomfortably, "ol' Grrff thinks maybe
we threw such a scare into them Ximchaks, when we drove

them through the Luzar Pass, they'll still be running. What d'you think, big man?"

Ganelon did not look happy.

"Scares don't last forever," he observed somberly. "I think maybe Sir Azrak is right. Once the Ximchak survivors get back home to the land of the Gomps, they'll want to return in force, to erase their defeat with victory."

"Or vengeance," observed Sir Belery, gnawing on a cucumber.

Palensus Choy looked vaguely disturbed.

"I say, you chaps," he spoke up in a thin, quavering voice. "You don't suppose, do you, that those ruffians will take it into their heads to turn on Zaradon and attempt to destroy it, do you? My castle, you know. Atop Mount Naroob. Don't suppose they could have recognized me, do you, and thus have known I was helping to drive them from Valardus?"

"I don't know," said Ganelon. "Who's in charge of the castle while you're away from it?"

"Well, Chongrilar, of course. Not that he's good for much. Loyal, yes. Faithful to a fault. But—bright? Bit of a dunderhead, I fear—"

"Dunderhead is it?" burbled Ollub Vetch mischievously. "*Stone*head, I'd call him! Oh, har, har, har (wheeze), har!"

The others, not seeing the point of this joke, exchanged glances of polite mystification.

All except Xarda of Jemmerdy and Prince Erigon. The more wine the two imbibed, the more breathless and red of face the girl knight grew, while Prince Erigon grew ever more dreamy and poetic-looking. And about the time Sir Jaspodar, the doddering old Royal Steward, came tottering in with another two dozen bottles of good vintage, the Prince whispered something about "hot in here" and "stroll in the castle gardens," and the two stole out into the silver glory of the Falling Moon hand in hand.

The knights had one by one fallen asleep, and were taken to their beds by men of the Castle Guard. Palensus Choy and Ollub Vetch stayed up late, conversing with King Vergus and King Yemple; the old magician was becoming increasingly worried about the security of his enchanted mountaintop palace, which lay directly in the Ximchak's line of retreat through the Pass.

So deep in conversation were they that only Grrff the Xombolian noticed, an hour or two later, when the handsome young Prince and the vivacious girl knight of Jemmerdy came back into the Grand Hall out of the gardens, that they were still holding hands, and now both of them looked dreamy and poetic.

Grrff grinned a secret smile of satisfaction of himself, but said nothing.

Book Two

SILVERMANE AT ZARADON

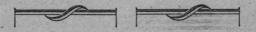

The Scene: The Mountains of Iriboth; the Jungles of Nimboland; the City of Urchak; Castle Zaradon.

New Characters: King Wunx and other Nimbolanders; Chongrilar the Stone Man; Eezik, Harooshk, Thurble, and other dwellers in Zaradon; quite a lot of Ximchaks.

8.

A Hasty Departure

Bright and early the very next morning, despite an aching head and an upset stomach, both brought on by his incautious indulgence in such nonimmortal practices as eating and drinking, Palensus Choy was anxious to make a hasty departure on Ishgadara in order to return to Zaradon, which was, he fancied, in momentary danger of being attacked by angry, vengeful Ximchaks.

Ganelon decided to go along because he wanted to see what the Ximchaks were, in fact, doing, and from the high vantagepoint of the mountaintop castle a good overview of the Horde's activity could be gained. He hadn't said much the night before, but it was gloomily obvious to him that their little skirmish in the Valley of Valardus was just that—a skirmish. The Ximchaks were not going to give up quite *that* easily, he guessed. And they would be down on Valardus, and in strength, once Kan Zar Kan had moved on and was no longer blocking the mouth of the Luzar Pass.

"Guess ol' Grrff'll go along too, big man," grumbled that stalwart, hefting his ygdraxel suggestively. "Never know when another pair o' strong arms'll come in handy."

"Excellent, excellent, glad to have you, I'm sure," mumbled Palensus Choy distractedly. "Plenty of room on dear Ishgadara's back for all of us. A bit crowded, though, if you intend coming along, m'dear," he said apologetically to Xarda.

"Oh, that's all right," said the girl knight vaguely. "I guess I'll be staying here with Erigon—*Prince* Erigon, I mean! His father has put us—*him*—in charge of estimating the damage done to the valley farms by the invasion, and of luring our—I mean, *his*—tenant farmers out of the hills, now that the danger has passed. We might join you later, in the

49

flying kayak, if Erigon—*Prince* Erigon—thinks it best. , . ."

Ganelon wrinkled up his brow and exchanged a puzzled glance with Griff, who snickered. It certainly wasn't like the snippy-tempered girl knight to be, well, quite this starry-eyed, or to yield the leadership of any expedition to the wishes of another. Something seemed to have come over her, but Silvermane, in his innocence, couldn't make out what it was.

"Quite all right, my dear, hah, hah, could we get started now, you chaps?" muttered the magician, nervously.

So they bid a brief farewell to King Vergus and his knights, climbed aboard the Gynosphinx, helped pull fat, wheezing King Yemple up between her mighty shoulders, and flew up into the morning freshness. The wind hissed through the bronze feathers of the female monster's strong wings, and as it was clear and cold, it soon dispelled their cobwebs, if not the butterflies in Choy's stomach.

Briefly, they touched down at Kan Zar Kan, where Slioma and Zilth and the other Kan Zar Kanians were growing restive, and anxious to be off. The City was all revved up, its engines idling, anxious to begin the return journey to a nice situation centrally located amid the Purple Plains, where it longed from the depths of its menchanical heart to take up the stable, normal, everyday life of an ordinary—and stationary—city.

As Kan Zar Kan was eager to be off, Ganelon and Grrff made their goodbyes brief. A hug and a kiss for bright-eyed Slioma, a few words for their friends among the former Iomagoths, a hasty promise to drop by sometime on their return trip to YamaYamaLand, and they were ready to go.

Except for Kurdi.

The little gypsy boy hung back reluctantly while the goodbyes were being made, then flung himself into Ganelon's arms, sobbing into his chest, mumbling inarticulate pleas.

"But, Kurdi, we can't take you with us," protested Ganelon awkwardly. "You belong here, with your folks—"

"Don't have no folks, 'm' a orphint," the boy sobbed.

"With your friends, then—"

"Don't have no friends. Wanna have adventures an' see th' world, an' be your squire," the boy said tearfully.

"But a warrior doesn't need—ah, hum, well," said Ganelon, letting his words trail away into silence, for, of course, warriors in Gondwane did have squires, just as did the wandering knights in the Middle Ages.

Grrff came to the awkward giant's rescue, scooping up the boy in his arms, making soothing, purring sounds deep in his throat, carrying him off to a far corner of the tier to dry his tears and tickle and tease him into cheerfulness again. Ganelon looked distinctly uncomfortable; not being able to do what other people wanted him to do always upset him. He wanted to say goodbye to the bright, eager little boy, for whom he had developed a powerful fondness—probably because Kurdi reminded him of little Phadia, his friend back in Shai. But Kurdi was nowhere to be found when it came time to leave.

They mounted up again, this time without fat King Yemple, waved a last farewell to their friends, and flew up from Kan Zar Kan toward the mountains. The glittering metal metropolis was already underway, gliding with a humming sound over the grassy floor of the valley, dwindling into a shining mote far amid the Purple Plains. Soon it was entirely lost to view.

Ishgadara bore them across the Valley of Valardus, which was like a huge notch cut by a giant out of the rampartlike wall of the Carthazian Mountains, toward the tall cleft in the end of the Valley which was the Luzar Pass.

Soon they went skimming down the Pass, with sheer cliff-walls of smooth stone soaring up to either side of them against the azure sky.

The Pass wove like a serpent's trail through the mountains, eventually giving forth on a broad country of rolling, tree-clad hills. The trees grew thicker and denser and the country became wilder and wilder the longer they flew. Now they were over the jungle country of Nimboland, many hours' march from Valardus, and still there was no sign of the Ximchaks who had survived the decimation of their strength by Kan Zar Kan.

"The jungle town of Urchak isn't far up that river there," puffed Ollub Vetch, pointing at a waterway which wove like a gleaming silvery ribbon through the thick jungles. "It's there that the Grand Chief of the Nimbolander tribesmen holds his court. I guess *he'll* know if the surviving Ximchaks came this way."

"I suppose you're right," murmured Palensus Choy nervously. "We might as well ask, anyway."

Urchak was a crude jungle settlement in the center of a large section of cleared ground, built on both sides of the

Nimbo River, which came winding down out of the Iriboth
Mountains farther north. The town consisted of about sixty
huts made mostly of bamboo, but there were a few larger
structures built of logs, and a triple palisade wall of logs
buried in the earth which encircled the entire jungle town
like a battlement, built to keep in their domesticated beasts.
Breaks in the wall allowed the river to wander right through
the village.

In the middle of the town rose a fairly imposing, though
primitive, two-story building of mixed log-and-bamboo work,
which was the residence of the Nimbolander monarch, King
Wutz, or Grand Chief Wutz, to give him his proper title.
Toward this structure Ishgadara directed her flight, coming
to earth before Wutz's front door.

The Nimbolanders scattered squealing in all directions as
the gigantic winged sphinx came settling down to earth in
their town square, but soon they came creeping back to peer
interestedly at the strangers from around the corners of their
huts. Choy coaxed them out with some magic tricks which
made them forget their panic and soon put them all in a
good humor.

They were an odd-looking bunch, not entirely human, but
close enough so that it didn't matter very much.* They *did*
look peculiar, though, what with their bright-blue skins and
pink eyes, their heads topped with great, frizzled masses of
woolly hair in which they wore carved ivory ornaments. Besides these ornaments, they didn't wear much—wooden
beads around their necks, wooden rings around their ankles
or wrists, and long grass skirts. They had no noses; instead,
they breathed through small orifices in their abdomens, where
the lungs were located.

The visitors to Nimboland had dismounted from Ishgadara's broad back, and were engaged in coaxing out the
timid junglemen, when Ganelon to his vast surprise espied

---

*By the period of Ganelon Silvermane, which was in the last
century before the close of the Eon of the Falling Moon, the human race *per se* was in a distinct minority, and *Homo sapiens*
shared the Supercontinent with many semihuman or quasihuman
or pseudohuman races, and quite a few that were thoroughly nonhuman. Among these, for example, were the Tigermen of Karjixia,
the Pseudowomen of Chuu, the Talking Heads of Soorm, the Red
Amazons, the Death Dwarves, the Mandragons of Mantragon, the
nigh-legendary Minimals, and the Merfolk and river-nixes. The
Nimbolanders were human enough, surely.

a familiar face peeping out from behind the scabrous bole of an immense marganzilla tree.

It was a small boy with thick black hair, brown skin, plump red cheeks, and flashing eyes, also black. He wore red tights on his slender legs, and a short heraldic jerkin, somewhat threadbare. There was a smudge on one cheek and tearstains beneath both eyes.

"Kurdi? Is that you?" rumbled the giant incredulously.

The boy essayed a wavering, uncertain smile, not at all sure he wouldn't be spanked. Then when Ganelon and Grrff exchanged huge grins, and began chuckling, the boy sighed with relief and hurled himself into their arms, hugging both of them furiously, being patted and clucked over.

"Jus' *couldn't* stay ahind!" he explained, breathlessly. "Wanna have adwentures too—"

"Ad*ven*tures," Ganelon corrected him absently. During their stay in Kan Zar Kan, both he and the Xombolian Tiger-man had taken quite a liking to the bright, inquisitive lad, and had formed the habit of correcting his speech. They now did so without being aware of it.

"But how did you—"

"Me carry um," Ishgadara grinned hugely, displaying square tusklike molars. The lady sphinx reared back on her lionlike hindlegs and made a cradling gesture with her front paws. "Li'l cub wanna come 'long, so me carry um. You no notice, hah? Ishgadara ferry smart, no?"

"Very smart, yes," said Grrff, with his growling laugh. "Now Grrff understands why you landed, just now, on your hind end first, nearly tipping us out of our seats."

Kurdi stole into Ganelon's arms, gazing up at the huge bronze champion shyly.

"Mad at Kurdi?" the boy whispered cajolingly.

Ganelon tried to look stern. Failing, he tousled the boy's black curls affectionately.

"Don't know what we'll do you with you, but I guess it'll be all right," he smiled.

And so the Hero of World's End acquired his squire.

And now they were six. Counting Ishgadara, of course!

9.

King Wunx Answers

While these things were happening, Palensus Choy was luring the Nimbolanders out of their huts and from behind trees with some harmless magic—turning a cookpot into a giant cabbage, then into a pink quarasch*, that sort of thing.

Ollub Vetch, not to be outdone, whipped some fancy fireworks from his pouch, and soon filled the beaten-earth square before the Grand Chief's hut with spinning wheels of purple and orange sparks, clouds of fragrant green and yellow smoke, and crimson zigzags. In no time, the savages were standing in a huge ring about their visitors, oohing and ahing, laughing and clapping delightedly.

Ollub Vetch topped off his performance by building a fire-fountain, nine tiers tall, which flashed through different colors, soared in a tall pillar of sparkling fire, then burst into a drifting shower of flower-shaped, sizzling fireballs. These exploded about the heads of the Nimbolanders harmlessly, leaving pleasantly perfumed streamers of colored smoke.

In less time that it has taken me to describe it, the absent-minded magician and the fat, puffing little inventor had made friends with the shy jungle-dwellers.

Theirs was a curious history, as Ollub Vetch explained to Ganelon, Kurdi, and Grrff, while Palensus Choy made pa-laver with the village elders. Originally jungle savages, they had undergone a wholesale conversion to Jingoism a few

---

*A kind of enormous praying mantis, very intelligent and quite friendly, which commonly inhabits the Meadowlands of Shyx. The quarasch, which looks intensely solemn, is a natural-born clown, delights in playing tricks, antics, puns, and the like. In the lands and nations of Greater Zuavia, a clown or court jester is commonly called a quarasch.

generations before, having been shown the error of their ways by peripatetic missionaries from Wazuzu. With the apotheosis of the Prophet Jingo, his ninety-nine disciples were dispatched to all corners of Zuavia. The pacifistic tenets of the Jingoist faith found little favor outside of Nimboland, and today (not counting the Holy City of Wazuzu itself, of course), the Church of Jingo the Revelator was thoroughly extinct.

Fortunately for the missionaries, the Nimbolanders had never been all that terribly belligerent, anyway. The peace-loving doctrines of the Revelator suited them just fine. Therefore they were by this time quite fully civilized, and disposed to be friendly to strangers, and nowhere near as ferocious and warlike as they appeared. In fact, as Ollub Vetch confided, they were excessively timid and quite ignorant of not only of the customs of war, but also of the use of weapons, the very concept of fighting having been forgotten a generation after their conversion. Luckily for them, the jungles of Nimboland were empty of any animals more dangerous than a species of black rabbit which grew to the size of a sheepdog and was clever enough to barter edible nuts, fruits, and berries for cabbages cultivated by the tribesmen. Their neighbors in the kingdoms of Ordovoy and Beldossa, to the east and the west respectively, got along well with them without any trouble, being, if anything, even more timid than the semi-intelligent rabbits.

At length King Wunx was coaxed out of his royal hut. He was immensely tall and incredibly thin and unbelievably old; his long, bony visage seamed into ten tousand wrinkles so that you could hardly find his eyes and had to guess where his mouth was. Despite this, he was painted and bedizened in a manner of such ferocity that you would have sworn he was a headhunter, if not actually a cannibal, an impression furthered by the number of skulls hung around his neck, wrists, ankles, and waist, which clanked hollowly together with every step. Only on closer examination could you notice, with relief, that these were not human skulls. (They were, in fact, the skulls of particularly large fieldmice which had died of old age.)

Once it had penetrated his dim and hazy old brain that his visitors were friends of the kindly and benign Immortal of Zaradon, the Grand Chief quaveringly insisted on serving them lunch. The meal consisted of vegetables, fruit, nuts, berries, stewed cabbages, beans, edible roots, and a variety

of river seaweed which, when toasted, was spicy and delicious—and also, of course, pre-salted.

The Nimbolanders, it seemed, were vegetarians as well as
pacifists. They had, it turned out, elaborated the tenets of
the Jingoist religion to their logical extremities. If it was
counter to the wishes of Hibbish—supreme divinity of the
Jingoistic pantheon—that they should hunt and kill either
animals or men, it seemed to them glaringly obvious that
these anti-slaughterous prohibitions should also include meat
creatures of any kind, including fish and insects. Fruits and
vegetables, obviously, were spiritually inferior and fitting and
proper food, as even the timid creatures of field and forest
devoured them in their primal innocence.

The vegetarian luncheon was all mixed together in a thick,
creamy, deliciously spicy gumbo, which the visitors found
very much to their liking. All of them, that is, except for
Grrff. The Karjixian, like his remote feline ancestors, was a
carnivore. It went against his grain to eat what he sneeringly
referred to as "green stuff" and "rabbit food."

In a feeble, quavering voice, so thin they could hardly
make it out, King Wunx replied to their questions concerning
the Ximchaks. A large party of five thousand or so of these
Barbarians had, he confirmed, come down from the Mountains of Iriboth to the northwest some months before. After
chasing away timid parties of curious Nimbolanders, and
laying waste to a village or two, they journeyed farther
south to the place where the Luzar Pass made a notch in the
towering ramparts of the Carthazian Mountains. And without any of the usual looting, burning, pillaging, and associa-
ated unfriendlinesses that generally go along with Barbarian
invasions. This seemed a bit odd to Ganelon, but Grrff suggested a theory that explained it quite adequately.

"Reckon the war party wuz sent on ahead to sound out
the country and see if'n it were dangerous," he grumbled,
scratching his hairy muzzle with one black claw. "Finding out
that these here Nimbolanders are harmless, the fighters went
on down to see how sticky things would be in Valardus, beyond the Pass. There they musta got caught up in the siege
—you know, big man, them Barbarians just can't resist a
good fight."

"I suppose you're right," nodded Silvermane.

"Why they goin' south, anyhow?" chirped Kurdi interestedly.

"Anyway," said Ganelon.

"Why *are* they going," said Grrff, simultaneously.

"From what I understand," mused Palensus Choy abstractedly, "a Warlord of extraordinary military genius has but recently risen to their helm (if a Horde can be said to have a helm, that is). This fellow—Zaar, they call him—is obviously looking for greener pastures, so to speak. The Thirty Cities of the Gompish Regime stood forth against his depredations quite stoutly, I believe. But there's nothing of much consequence south of Gompia until you get across the Purple Plains and into the northern parts of Yama-YamaLand."

"Hoy," puffed Ollub Vetch, nodding vigorously. "These bully boys like a good fight, as our Xombolian friend observed a moment ago. Since Nimboland will be a pushover, and so will its neighboring realms of Ordovoy and Beldossa, who have precious little history of wars or invasions, and since Valardus is famously unwarlike, there's nothing much up here to offer them what they're looking for. Down south in YamaYamaLand, begob, they'll find plenty to keep them busy. The Red Enchantress—not to mention the green horrors of Dwarfland! Even the Realm of the Nine Hegemons!"

Ganelon looked unhappy. The Hegemony was the only homeland he had ever known, although he had not exactly been born there, never having actually been born at all,* as far as he was aware of, and he was disturbed by the idea that soon the tremendous and warlike Ximchak Horde might descend upon the peaceful nations of YamaYamaLand.

"Yes, yes," murmured Palensus Choy. "But, even more recently, some remnants of the ruffian band must have passed through Nimboland on their way back to rejoin their friends in the Gompish country. Is it not so, King Wunx?"

The decrepit jungle monarch champed his toothless jaws, which oozed a drool of spittle, and blinked his rheumy old eyes, as if by these processes to stimulate the actions of his memory.

At length the old geezer quaveringly affirmed the accuracy

---

*Ganelon Silvermane was a Construct, an android superman, tailored to some gigantic endeavor he had yet to discover, by an extinct race of omniscient beings called the Time Gods. Grown to physical maturity in stasis, he emerged from the Time Vault under the ruined city of Ardelix, to be adopted by a wandering Godmaker and his wife, on their way to Zermish in the Hegemony. See my redaction of the First Book of the Epic, *The Warrior of World's End*.

of the statement made to him by the Immortal of Zaradon.

"Oh, ah," he wheezed feebly. "They gert hairy brutes did
pass by this way, aye, 'twar early yester-even'n', er late night,
hit war."

"Indeed. Ahem, and which way did they go?" inquired the
absent-minded magician.

"Dew north, hit war, dew north," cackled the jungle pa-
triarch. "Rather beat-hup, they wuz, tew, har har. Reckon
as haow they Valardines done whupped 'em, snort!" Then,
suddenly recollecting the pacifistic dogmas of his faith, the
decrepit oldster assumed a pious expression. "Pore benighted
heathen," he added lamely.

Palensus Choy paled.

"*Due* north, you say?"

"Oh, ah. Aye. Toward them Iribothy Mountings, straight
fer Mount Narooby, hit war."

"Oh, my," groaned Choy hollowly.

Mount Naroob. Toward Mount Naroob the three thousand battered survivors of Kan Zar Kan's massacre had
headed, according to the Grand Chief of Nimboland.

Naroob was directly north of the jungle town of Urchak.

And the magician's palace of Zaradon was built on the top
of Naroob. . . .

10.

Marvels of Zaradon

As soon as they could, in decency, depart without causing insult to the hospitality of the Nimbolanders, they did so. Mounting the Gynosphinx, with little Kurdi seated before them at the base of Ishgadara's neck, the adventurers took to the air and flew north across the jungleland into the Mountains of Iriboth.

Before very long, Mount Naroob appeared directly ahead of them, her pinnacle looming above the clouds. Castle Zaradon clung to the topmost spire of the moutain, a cluster of slender minarets whose onion-shaped upper works, plated in cinnabar-red, caught the sunlight.

Silvermane, whose only previous experience with an enchanter's palace had been with the Illusionist's own citadel of Nerelon, looked about him interestedly as they approached the sparkling structure. The walls and towers looked as if cut from snowy white quartz, glittering with mica. A rooftop garden dripped with greenery, the verdure hanging down the milky walls like a merman's beard. The swelling globe of one fat dome gleamed with coppery fire amid the upthrusting spears of the slim, bulb-tipped spires.

There was no doorway opening out onto the mountaintop, and the only way you could enter Zaradon was from the air. Choy directed the Gynosphinx to land atop the parapet of the walls which encircled the central dome and its minarets. There the travelers found themselves on a broad and level thoroughfare of smooth stone whose outer circuit was crenelated into an effect like that of battlements.

"Welcome, welcome," murmured the Immortal, vaguely gesturing. At his approach a portal of sparkling brass appeared in the sleek quartzy wall; thereby they entered, finding themselves upon a narrow balcony which ran around the upper story of a deep hall of enormous breadth and extent. Far above their heads, fluted pillars of dark-green malachite supported the copper dome. They descended by a marble staircase to the main hall, where tall-backed chairs of carven wood encircled a firepit in which danced magic flames of tangerine, canary, pale gold and bloody crimson.

His back set against the nearest malachite pillar, a huge statue of carven granite, shaped like a nude man, stood facing the pit of dancing flames. This figure Palensus Choy now addressed, somewhat to their surprise.

"Chongrilar, I say, have we been invaded at all?"

Even more to their surprise, the statue answered this query.

"A par-rty of nomad war-rior-rs circled past the base of Naroob but early this morn-ning, master, but continued on into Gompland," said the statue.

Grrff jumped and swore, nape-fur bristling at this marvel. Even Ganelon looked startled. Noticing their stares, the fat little inventor chuckled.

"Hoy!" he snorted apologetically. "You must forgive our absent-minded host! This is Chongrilar, the Stone Man, Choy's major-domo and general factotum. Chongy, give greeting to Grrff the Xombolian, Ganelon Silvermane, and small Kurdi."

The statue lumbered into motion, stepping away from the malachite column, and approached them on slow, heavy feet. It moved with a grating of stone rubbing against stone, and although they stared with fascination, they could not discern how what seemed like stiff and solid stone could flex and bend.

The Stone Man greeted them solemnly, one by one. Its face was rather manlike, but stylized like bad municipal sculpture on public monuments, staring eyes under a broad brow crowned with crisp, curled hair carved in an antique style, and the rest of its face of a severe, "classical" and rather standard beauty.

"Grreet-tings, and welcome to Zarr-a-don," said the Stone Man, in a heavy, ponderous, slow, and rasping voice that burred the sound of 'r' and separated bisyllabic words into carefully enunciated syllables.

They greeted the magically animated statue awkwardly, rather happy that the creature did not offer to shake hands. The very notion of having their hands clasped in those heavy hands of stone made them wince.

While Chongrilar stalked off into the recesses of the hall to fetch the mail that had come for his master during his absence from Zaradon, Palensus Choy explained off-handedly that the Stone Man was the only successful result of a series of experiments he had conducted a dozen millennia ago to embue stone with life.

"Once charged with vital energy," the magician said absently, "Chongrilar seems to be as immortal as I, unaging, of course, and exceptionally durable to wear and tear. He makes a splendid chamberlain for me and runs my household admirably, although a bit too ponderous to negotiate floors or staircases of anything else but solid stone. He weighs five tons, you know."

Chongrilar reappeared clutching a sheaf of letters in one stone hand, while supporting a copper tray of spicy beverages and candied refreshments in the other. With slow, dragging steps the animated statue served these while Choy leafed rapidly through the mail, tossing advertising circulars and pleas for charitable donations into the firepit.

After finishing their drinks, Chongrilar showed the visitors to their rooms while Palensus Choy and Ollub Vetch went into another chamber called the observatorium to use the Immortal's magic crystal for scrying. Choy was interested to see where the remnants of the Ximchak besiegers had gotten to.

While the enchanted palace of Zaradon was large enough, only a few rooms were outfitted for the housing of guests, and one of these was already inhabited by Ollub Vetch. So, while the Tigerman took the smaller of the remaining two, Ganelon had to share his bed with little Kurdi.

Poking his small snub nose inquisitively into everything, since almost everything was new and exciting to the boy, Kurdi stumbled upon the bathroom. This imposing and sybaritic chamber contained an incredible sunken bath of brown marble, with hot and cold running water, jets of perfumed air, and all manner of other luxuries which the bright-eyed boy found entrancing. As soon as Chongrilar explained in his ponderous gloomy way how everything worked, Kurdi wasted no time in stripping down to the buff and jumping into the steaming tub.

With an indulgent smile, Ganelon watched the boy wriggle voluptuously through huge mountains of scented pink bubbles, frolicking delightedly in a bath big enough for both of

them to share. While the little boy splashed and cavorted to
his heart's content, happily lathering bare brown limbs in the
sweet-smelling suds, Ganelon, having stored away his personal gear, went forth to find his companions. Becoming lost
in the labyrinthine ways of the many-leveled palace, he
found himself in a long hall peopled by remarkable beings,
all of them alive, and all of them unbelievable.

Ishgadara hailed him hoarsely from her stall at the end.

"These peingk my friends," the lady sphinx said. "This pe
Harooshk." Ganelon could not help staring: Harooshk was
about fifteen feet tall—or long, depending on whether he
was standing up or lying down—and most of his fifteen feet
were dragon, greenish-black scales and barb-tipped tail and
jagged spine and all. The last part of him, his head, was more
human than dragon, except that his elongated nose was
almost a snout and his grinning mouth revealed blunt,
rounded fangs. His huge, unblinking lidless eyes were like
bright gold coins; he had a beard and mane and mustache of
snaky green tendrils, all twisted together.

He was a Mandragon, of course. Ganelon greeted him
lamely, not quite knowing how to pass the time of day with
a creature he had always considered to be fabulous and myth-
ical, but doing his best. Harooshk grinned shyly, showing
the tip of his long barbed tongue, and emitted a brief jet of
live steam by way of returning the greeting. His smell was
a peculiar blend of snaky muskiness and hot sulfur, not entirely displeasing.

"And this be Eezik," rumbled Ishgadara.

Eezik was a Great White Youk, tall, skinny, long-legged,
all greasy-white from top to toe, crested with an immense
crown of branching antlers. Eezik honked a polite greeting,
not being capable of speech, and offered to shake Ganelon's
hand in his own three-fingered paw. Ganelon did not feel
quite as uncomfortable meeting Eezik as he had when introduced to Harooshk, for his own master, the Illusionist, had
kept a domesticated Youk at Nerelon.

"This Thurple," said Ishgadara. Unable to pronounce the
letter 'b,' she meant "Thurble."

Thurble turned out to be a creature quite new to Ganelon,
which he later understood to be a Pyrosprite. Akin to the
Fire-Elementals, Thurble resembled a diminutive, potbel-
lied, spindly-legged little manlike being, translucent to the
eye, and glowing redly with heat. Small flames crackled in
his wiry bronze-colored beard, and smoke wisps dribbled

from the corners of his wide-lipped mouth. His kennel was lined with woven asbestos mats. They did not shake hands.

"Is that all of them?" inquired Ganelon. Ishgadara shrugged burly, furry shoulders.

"Mantichore moultingk now, no feel friendly," she advised. "Andt Piast hipernatingk."

Ganelon said nothing, but felt secretly relieved. It was unsettling enough to meet Mandragons or Youks or Pyrosprites on a friendly social footing, but he drew the line at Piasts. Piasts were milk-white lake-dwelling serpents six hundred feet long.

Returning to the room he shared with Kurdi, Silvermane found the boy out of the sunken bath at last, toasting his wet brown legs in jets of hot, perfumed air, giggling delightedly.

"Dry yourself off now, Kurdi, and put some clothes on," he ordered. "We have to find our way back to where the others are."

Reluctantly quitting the sybaritic pleasures of the bathing chamber, whose utter novelty entranced him,* Kurdi scampered over to the closet and started trying on a variety of garments obviously produced by magic with him and Ganelon in mind. For his uses the magician had created a number of pairs of tights and tabards, and some loose, cool tunics that were of sleek, silky weave, and only came down to the upper thigh, leaving his long legs bare. At least, Kurdi *thought* they were tunics, but so short were they that the magician probably had it in mind that he should wear them as blouses, with tights underneath.

Exposed on its mountainous height to the cold gale-force winds, Zaradon was kept heated to tropic temperatures. For this reason Kurdi finally settled on a skimpy loincloth of red silk, originally intended as a largish handerchief.

With Kurdi, after a fashion, dressed, Ganelon was ready to set out on a second expedition to find his way back to the main hall. But this time Palensus Choy sent Chongrilar the Stone Man to escort them down to an emergency meeting so he didn't have to try to find his way unaided.

---

*Being a true Iomagoth born and bred, the little boy had probably never taken a bath before in all of his eleven years, hence the "novelty."

11.

The Ximchaks Turn Back

Scrying had revealed to Palensus Choy that the remnants of the Barbarians who had laid siege to Valardus had not returned to the Gompish country after all. Only a small part of the surviving force had threaded a path through the Iribothian Mountains, back to the felt tents of their people.

The bulk of the survivors had circled the base of Mount Naroob and gone north, encamping at the head of the canyon which led through the mountain range into Gompland. Soon even those few messengers who had gone on into the Gomp country returned, and with three thousand unmounted warriors fresh from the main encampment of the Horde. Now they were turning about and retracing their route— back toward Mount Naroob and the enchanted castle on its peak.

"I knew I should have laid a spell of invisibility on Zaradon before we left to look into things at Valardus," sighed Palensus Choy, combing his long thin beard with nervous fingers. "On their way back home they must have spied it, for Zaradon is only clearly seen at night, when the night wind blows away the mists which enwreath the mountain."

The next day the vision-crystal in Choy's observatorium showed an even grimmer picture. The Ximchak force, now several thousand strong, was camping in a huge circle around the base of the mountain, and exploratory parties were already out, scouting the steep sides of Naroob to find the best path to the mountain's crest. It could no longer be doubted that the Barbarians knew the role Palensus Choy had played in their resounding defeat before the fire-moat of Valardus, and were embarked upon a mission of vengeance.

They were not very smart, thought Ganelon Silvermane

to himself. Of course, being Barbarians in the first place meant they weren't civilized, and that implied a certain lack of smartness anyway. Civilized armies know better than to try to pick fights with powerful magicians.

It would take the besiegers quite some time to reach the crest of the mountain, for its sides were steep and precipitous in the extreme. He got busy organizing the defenses of Zaradon. What there were of them, that is.

"You mean you have no fighters?" asked Ganelon in surprise. Most magicians of Palensus Choy's class had quite a number of ways to defend themselves against attackers. But the absent-minded Immortal, it seemed, had never visualized the need and had not prepared for it.

"None, I fear," Choy murmured absently, peering into the luminous globe of the scrying glass.

"No automatons, or ghost servants, or captive genies?" inquired Silvermane. The old magician shook his head sadly.

"Nothing at all that can fight?"

Choy shrugged. "Well, my boy, the animals, of course. In the menagerie. But they are all tame and I wouldn't care to risk their lives, you know. I regard them as my friends. . . ."

"Hoy," puffed Ollub Vetch, hitching his chair forward, "'tis a fortunate thing for us, Zaradon hath no portals which open on the first tier."

"That is so," mused Silvermane grimly. For neither door nor window broke the smooth, cliffy walls of the first story of Castle Zaradon.

"Grrff thinks it won't stop 'em for long," grumbled the Tigerman. "All they'll need to reach the second tier is siege ladders, eh, big man?"

Ganelon said nothing; obviously, Grrff was correct. If the Barbarians reached the mountaintop, it was only a matter of time before they could effect an entry into Zaradon, despite its fortifications.

"Well," wheezed the fat little inventor, comfortingly. "Leastways we can harry them a little. Master Silvermane, what were the formula for them explosives Kan Zar Kan made up for you, do you remember? With a goodly supply of such, mounted astride our trusty Ishgadara, we can render *rather* hazardous their ascent of Mount Naroob."

"Well, if you think you can brew some of the stuff," said Ganelon dubiously. "Let me see, now: there was some soft stuff in it, like talcum, only yellow, bright yellow, and it smelled terrible—"

"Like rotten eggs, were it?" demanded the fat little man, eyes snapping excitedly. At Silvermane's nod, he said, "Aha! Sulfur, I'll warrant! Go on, m'boy, go on."

"And some soft, crumbly dry stuff, very black."

"Hmm! Graphite, mebbe . . . How did the City make the stuff, d'you recall at all?"

Ganelon rubbed his lantern jaw, as if thereby to somehow stimulate his powers of recollection.

"The City had the Iomagoths gather sticks of wood, which it then burned in ovens," he said slowly. "I don't mean they set the wood afire, but sort of roasted it, or toasted it—"

"Charcoal?" mused Ollub Vetch. "Well, mebbe so . . . anything else, m'boy?"

Ganelon tried to think, wrinkling up his brows with effort. "Something else . . . salt."

Vetch blinked without comprehension.

"Salt?"

"Well, some kind of salt. Salt-something, the City called it . . . I think it was 'salt.' Maybe it was 'sal' . . ."

"Sal ammoniac?"

"No."

"Salicylic acid?"

"No."

"It weren't salol, were it? White crystalline stuff, produced by the action of salicylic acid on phrenol?"

"I don't think so."

"Sal volatile?"

"No . . ."

"It weren't no herb, were it? Y'know, m'boy, plants, like? Salvia, or salep, salsify, or salmonberry?"

"No."

Ollub Vetch stuffed the end of his mustache into his mouth and chewed thereupon in an agony of frustration, eyes squinched shut in furious thought. From time to time he would mutter something half-aloud: "Sal soda, otherwise known as sodium carbonate?" "Salicin?" "Salpa?" But to each of these mutters Silvermane would reply with a negative monosyllable.

Chongrilar the Stone Man shuffled his feet, making the stone flags squeal. The animated statue, who had charge of the castle kitchens, along with almost everything else, spoke up in his solemn, melancholy way:

"Not salma-gundi, I sup-pose, Mast-ter?"

The little fat man fixed the statue with a glare that would

have sizzled anything less durable than granite. "Salmagundi," said Vetch through his teeth, "is chopped meat mixed with onions, eggs, and anchovies. Be serious, Clunkhead!"

Looking even more lugubrious than usual, Chongrilar went over to stir up the fire, while Vetch, with a snort of impatience, hopped out of his chair.

"Well, nothing to do but try them all, and anything else that occurs t'me," he said briskly. "Friend Choy, I assume it will be all right with you if I require the uses of your alchemical laboratorium for a time?"

"Eh? Oh. Certainly, my dear fellow," murmured Palensus Choy with a vague gesture. "Chongrilar will show you the way . . . *Do* try not to break anything, there's a good chap!"

"That I can*not* promise," huffed the fat inventor. "The vapors released by this admixture of elements would seem to expand with excessive vigor, but I will strive to confine them to sturdy vessels." He went waddling off in the wake of the animated granite statue, rubbing his hands together briskly.

Choy stroked his tall brow with restless fingers. He looked perturbed about something, as was, after all, only natural when you consider that his enchanted citadel was about to suffer the attack of several thousand howling primitives. But the expression on his gentle, amiable features was not precisely one of worry: it was more the look of one who has forgotten something important, which he is trying to remember. After a time, lost in thought, he went wandering off into his own suite of rooms, leaving Ganelon and Grrff and little Kurdi to their own devices.

A little before supper they were startled by a dull explosion. Tumbling over each other, Palensus Choy and Ganelon and Kurdi, with the lumbering Stone Man bringing up the rear, burst into the laboratorium to find something fizzling and spitting bright sparks in a frying pan suspended over a low fire. It emitted, along with the sizzling, popping sparks, a remarkably stenchful black vapor.

At their entry, Ollub Vetch looked up from dreamy-eyed contemplation of the hissing, stinking mess in the iron pan. His face was covered with black soot and small sparks smoldered in his mustachios, but the expression on his fat visage was one of bliss.

"It was saltpeter," he sighed happily.

"Oh," said Ganelon.

"I tried 'em all," he grinned, gesturing at rows of identical pans filled with unappetizing-looking glop. "Nothing reacted with the charcoal and the sulphur save this. Saltpeter. Potassium nitrate."

He fixed the lanky magician with a look blissfully eloquent of a determination to conclude once and for all their long-simmering feud over the comparable supremacy of science and sorcery. Then he looked over at Silvermane, bright eyes inquisitive in the sooty mask of his face.

"I don't suppose," he said tentatively, "that you recollect the, ah, *proportions?*"

Ganelon looked uncomfortable, and shook his head reluctantly. "I had no reason to ask about them, you know," he explained.

"Ah, well. Just take a little longer, as it were," muttered the fat inventor with chagrin. "Now git out of here, all of you, and let an inventor invent!"

12.

Ollub Vetch Invents

For the next two days or so the Ximchaks tried to scale the sides of Mount Naroob, without making an easy job of it.

Palensus Choy had chosen his mountain with care, it seems. His prime consideration had been one of privacy, a condition conducive to magical studies, since magicians (even more than other folks) do not wish to be interrupted at their work, and so he had selected a mountain that was virtually impossible for anyone to climb on foot. Straight up and down, it was, or almost straight, anyway. As the Ximchaks did not take very long to discover. They would get about *this* far up, then find it humanly impossible to go any farther, and try off to the left or the right. As often as not, trying the left or the right made them slide back down the side of the mountain, sometimes hurried along by an avalanche or two.

More than a few assorted broken heads, arms, legs, and clavicles were the result.

But the Ximchaks were nothing if not persistent. They were filled with determination and driven by a sense of purpose that could best be described as "unrelenting." And eventually they did find a route to the top, although it took them days to get even halfway up, and more days than that to go all the way to the top.

During this time, nothing was seen or heard from Ollub Vetch. Nothing, that is, but occasional small explosions in the dim recesses of the palace; and these were generally followed by distant cries of "Drat!" or even stronger expletives.

To while away the time, there being not much else for them to do, Ganelon Silvermane and Grrff the Xombolian Tigerman went out two or three times a day to reconnoiter

69

from the air. They bestrode Ishgadara the sphinx-girl on
these reconnaissance trips, of course, since Istrobian's flying
kayak had remained back in Valardus with Prince Erigon
and the knightrix of Jemmerdy.

They could easily have followed the slow progress of the
invading Ximchaks through the magic vision viewing-crystal
in Palensus Choy's observatorium, of course. But Silvermane
was bored and restless from inactivity, and needed to be out
in the open air and *doing* something.

These aerial reconnaissance missions revealed that the
Ximchak Barbarians were slowly but steadily, and with grim
determination, conquering the steep sides of Mount Naroob.
More than two hundred were laid up with broken bones or
bandage-wrapped noggins by now, but every loss served but
to instill within them an even fiercer determination to make
it to the top.

It began to seem that absolutely nothing would or could
deter the Barbarians, who shook balled fists and waved their
weapons in a bellicose manner whenever they espied the pair
mounted astride the winged sphinx-girl (when they could
spare the use of one hand, that is, from the task of holding
onto the rock wall).

"Another day of this, and they'll be at our gates," noted
Silvermane to the Karjixian. "If we *had* gates, that is."

"A good thing they don't have wings or some manner of
flying vessels," grumbled Grrff.

Night and day Ollub Vetch toiled in the laboratory, making
sulfurous stenches, amazing messes, and—occasionally—loud,
fairly destructive bangs. These infrequent explosions shook
the windows and dirtied the ceilings, and to each muffled
boom from the near distance, Palensus Choy jumped and
winced and bit his fingernails.

"If only I could remember," the languid magician mumbled
to himself on these occasions.

"Remember *what,* master?" Kurdi chirped brightly.

The magician made a vague gesture.

"What it is about Zaradon that I seem to have forgotten."

That evening the fat inventor emerged from the seclusion
of the laboratorium, smeared with soot, part of his wispy
hair singed away on one side of his head, his clothing stained
with chemicals and eaten through, here and there, by powerful corrosives.

"No luck?" inquired Grrff.

"No luck," swore the inventor, fretfully gobbling a plate of sandwiches and sending Kurdi scampering off to the kitchens for some more wine.

"If only you had asked the *proportions*," grexed the fat little man with an accusatory glare at Ganelon Silvermane.

The bronze giant shrugged uncomfortably. "I had no particular reason to inquire about them," he repeated apologetically. The inventor's grumblings lapsed into thirsty gurglings just then, for Kurdi had fetched his wine.

At sunrise of the following day the first troops of the Ximchak appeared to view on the mountaintop. They stomped their booted feet and jumped up and down and blew on their fingers, for the wind was thrillingly cold at this height. Chongrilar took up a watch station atop the battlements of the first tier, and at intervals throughout the morning reported the successful ascent of yet more and more of the warriors, his dull voice melancholy and lugubrious.

"What's eating him?" Grrff grouched, after the latest statistics had come booming down into the great hall, dying in fading echoes. "He'd made of solid stone, and the Ximchaks can't hurt him nowise."

"Chongrilar is a peaceable and even-tempered fellow, for an animated eidolon," explained Palensus Choy absently. "He knows he will have to fight the ruffians, since, with the two of you, and perhaps dear Ishgadara, he is about the only resident of Zaradon who can fight. It makes the poor fellow rueful to contemplate such eventual violence."

"Oh, it does, does it?" growled Grrff testily. "Ol' Grrff'll rueful him somethin' rueful, if the lumphead doesn't pitch in, when the time comes, and hold up his own end!"

"I feel confident that the dear chap will do his part," mumbled Choy dimly. Then he jumped in his seat. "What's *that?*" he inquired in startled tones.

That was a really resounding thump which shook the walls and made the floor jump, like a miniature and momentary earthquake, much more effective than the occasional booms and bangs which kept emitting from Ollub Vetch in the laboratorium.

"Battering ram," said Ganelon Silvermane, remembering such siege devices from the defense of Zermish in which he had played so decisive a role during the invasion of the Indigons six months before.

"*Battering* rams?" repeated the Tigerman incredulously.

"Where'd they get battering rams? No trees grow up here; much too windy."

"They must have cut them in the jungles of Nimboland and hauled them up the sides of the mountains by ropes and winches."

Grrff scratched his hairy ears perplexedly. "Well, maybe so, big man. But howcum we never saw 'em while flying around on Ishgadara?"

"I don't know," admitted Silvermane. "Maybe they pulled them up at night, when we were asleep."

Another wall-shaking thump—ah—shook the walls, timed as if to emphasize his words.

"Anyhow, they've got them, all right," added Ganelon Silvermane grimly.

A third thump was followed by the noise of something falling in the next room, and made a couple of candles in the great hall pop out of their candlesticks onto the floor. Kurdi scampered to put them back in place and stamped out the smoldering carpet.

"Battering ram," growled the Karjixian, grabbing up his ygdraxel in one furry paw. "No wonder it took 'em five days to climb the mountain, if they had to lug siege equipment up the sides, as well."

"Oh dear, dear me!" whiffled Palensus Choy, slapping the arm of his chair fretfully. "If only I could recall to mind what it is about Zaradon that I have forgotten, all of this hurly-burly would not be necessary!"

"We'd better get to the walls and join the Stone Man," said Ganelon to Grrff, unlimbering the Silver Sword. "If they carried rams all this way, it's a cinch they thought to bring along some siege ladders, too."

"Dear me, dear me!" moaned Choy. "All this noise and confusion—"

Just then a deafening explosion sounded from the depths of the palace and the floor jumped underneath them and black clouds of stinking smoke wafted between the pillars. Ollub Vetch came tottering into view, his clothes burnt half off his tubby form, and the rest of him black with soot from head to foot.

"*Success!*" he cried, brandishing a smoking flagon triumphantly.

He had every right to feel triumphant, had Ollub Vetch. After all, he had just reinvented gunpowder!

13.

Four Against One Hundred

Supper hour or no supper hour, it was time to man the barricades, for, from the thumps and bumps made by the Ximchak battering rams, it seemed likely that the Barbarians would break through the doorless outer wall of the first tier of Zaradon before the world was very much older.

While Palensus Choy and little Kurdi followed Ollub Vetch back into the laboratorium to assist him in the preparation of explosives, Ganelon Silvermane and Grrff the Xombolian climbed the stairs to the top of the first tier and peered out through the crenelations to see what the Barbarian besiegers were up to.

They had rigged four long battering rams in rope cradles, and were swinging these in rhythm against a stretch of sparkling wall. Each ram consisted of a very long and very heavy treetrunk from which the branches and other protuberances, if any, had been removed, so that the logs were smooth on all sides. Both ends of these rams were capped with iron, or perhaps bronze—the dim glimmer of an almost extinguished sunset made it hard to tell which—so that the wood would not split from repeated impacts.

"Looks like they know their business," grumbled the Tigerman. Ganelon nodded but said nothing. *Thump, thump, thump,* went the rams, swinging in their ropy cradles from overhead A-shaped frames. At each thump the stone crumbled a little, beginning to break inward. Since the rams were at work on the very base of the walls, and since the walls supported the lofty heights of Castle Zaradon, the walls were exceptionally thick at this point. Still, it was just a matter of time.

"Shall we go down and knock 'em about a bit?" suggested

73

Grrff with a grin, hefting his ygdraxel. Chongrilar the Stone Man looked away pointedly, his sculptured face registering both fastidious disapproval and woeful gloominess. Ganelon looked over the hasty encampment the besiegers had thrown up—crude tents and flimsy huts.

"There be only about a hundred of 'em got up to the top yet," rumbled the Karjixian. "Between us, big man, and Granitehead over there, guess we can mess 'em up a bit. Whaddayou say?"

"If we're going to take them on at all, without the bombs, that is," Silvermane grunted, "we'd better do it now. By morning there'll be a thousand or more. But how do we get down to fight them?"

"On Ishgadara," said Grrff. "Hey, Lunkhead, go fetch her sphinxship, will you?"

Ishgadara landed them in the very midst of the ram teams. Piling off her broad back, the giant bronze man and the Karjixian sprang at the nearest Ximchaks, sunset flashing in the polished metal of Grrff's ygdraxel and Ganelon's huge broadsword.

The Ximchaks were burly-chested brown men, wrapped in furs, belted with black leather, adorned with odds and ends of steel or bronze armor. Most of them wore bushy beards curled into fat sausagelike ringlets, and around their thick brown throats, which were the hue of milk chocolate, hung miniature gold statuettes representing the major divinities of their savage pantheon. Some of them wore these figurines dangling from their pierced lobes, like large and rather long earrings. They seemed to be fully human, or almost fully human, at any rate, for their only discernible variation from the human norm was their eyes, which had irises of brilliant scarlet. This peculiarity was enhanced by their custom of painting wide green circles around their eyes before going to war.

Mounted astride their ornithohippi, as they had been at the siege of Valardus, they had appeared quite imposing. But now they were no longer mounted, since orniths are be-feathered quadrupeds—bird-horses, but more horse than bird, totally lacking wings—and, although agile and sure-footed as the proverbial mountain goat, would have found it impossible to scale so steep a mountain as Naroob. Now afoot, then, the Ximchaks revealed the fact that they were, most of them, less than five feet in height, with remarkably bowed legs from a lifetime spent in the saddle. Ganelon, Grrff, and Chongrilar, then, towered above them. Especially Ganelon, as the tallest of the Ximchaks scarcely stood higher than his navel, or would have, if he had one, which he didn't.*

The Silver Sword itself was longer than most of the Ximchaks were tall, and with the added length of Ganelon's long arms, gave him a reach the stunted little brown savages could not stand against. In no time he had dispatched six of them and the remainder of that particular ram team were running in blind rout. He turned to cut apart the A-frame and to chop into small pieces the ropes from which the battering ram hung suspended.

Grrff had polished off five or six more with his long-handled Karjixian weapon, and Chongrilar had gloomily caved in the skulls of five others impudent enough to come within the reach of his stony arms.

Chopping down the second ram from its supports, Grrff counted the corpses. "Sixteen dead and one about to give his last gasp," he announced with gruesome satisfaction. "Not bad for ten minutes' work, eh, big man?"

"I suppose not," said Silvermane in a noncommittal tone of voice. "Only about eighty-four more, and we'll be through," he added, nodding in the direction of the rude camp, where a snarling, cursing mob of savages was forming to rush them. There seemed to be an awful lot of the bowlegged little men, and the expressions on their chocolate-brown faces was anything but friendly.

Grrff, however, hadn't been in a good free-for-all for longer than he could recall. He spat into his palms, got a good tight grip on his ygdraxel, and eyed the angry savages with relish.

"Least we c'n do is meet 'em halfway," he suggested, grinning to show all of his long, pointed tiger-teeth. Ganelon agreed, and without further ado they charged the mob, which scattered in all directions, then gathered again into small clumps while the two cut into pieces those Ximchaks who hadn't decided until too late which way to run, and hence had to stand and fight.

Another four or five cadavers now littering the mountain-

---

*Ganelon Silvermane was not a true human but a synthetic man, an android, designed by the Time Gods for some ineluctable purpose, as I have previously mentioned.

top, the two warriors turned to find themselves surrounded by a growling, spitting ring of vengeful Ximchaks. Chongrilar, who had remained behind to break down the other battering rams, now looked up, saw his companions in their peril, and charged upon the Ximchaks from the rear. It took some time for the heavy Stone Man to get up enough speed, for, tipping the scales at five tons of solid stone, he wasn't exactly designed for sprinting. But when he *did* build up enough momentum, it was equally difficult for him to slow down.

He ran entirely through the dense ring of Ximchaks, knocking them head over heels, bowling them over like an express train crashing through a board fence. After trampling thirty-nine of the unfortunate savages underfoot, he burst out of the farther side of the circle and headed off across the plateau-smooth mountaintop. Unable to stop himself very easily, he was still lumbering at a fairly swiftish clip when he vanished in the darkness of the distance.

He had, at least, broken through the ring of Ximchaks. Now Grrff and Ganelon made for the wide hole he had made, weapons swinging. They burst out of the ring, Ximchaks falling to either side like ripe wheat stalks toppling before the scythelike sweeps of the Silver Sword and the dreaded Tigermanish weapon.

Their ranks considerably thinned, the Ximchaks regathered for a charge. At the castle wall, Ganelon and the Tigerman turned, set their backs against the stony barrier, and waited for the attack.

"Wantingk to go pack now?" inquired Ishgadara, lazily cleaning her immense paws. The Gynosphinx had played a minor role in the fight thus far, merely contenting herself with the crushing of a half-dozen or eight Ximchak skulls from behind, each head-busting blow being, from her point of view, only a half-playful slap. Ganelon shook his head.

"No, but you can join us, if you want to, Ishgadara," he said, just as the Ximchaks charged, yelling and hurtling spears.

She spread her wings and pounced, sailing into the forefront of the savage onslaught like a yellow boulder cast from a catapult. *Slap!—slap!—slap!* went her great paws, flicking out to either side, faster than the eye could follow, mere tawny blurs. Men fell with broken necks and shattered heads. Then she reared up on her hind legs, towering all of fifteen feet into the air, which made her nearly twice as tall as Ganelon. She waded through the yowling mob of bowlegged little warriors like a bull elephant through a herd of sheep, and her paws never stopped flailing. The mass of Ximchaks melted away from her like a plateful of ice cream from a blowtorch.

When the two caught up to her, the sphinx-girl was sitting atop a mound of corpses, interestedly licking the blood from her paws.

"Well, *that* narrows the odds a little!" said Grrff the Xombolian. The eleven Ximchaks still alive were dwindling in the distance as fast as their bowed legs could run.

They didn't run very far, however, for before Ganelon and the others had time to finish demolishing the remaining battering ram, Chongrilar's gloomy prediction came true. More Ximchaks had made the final assault on the peak, and, encountering their comrades in flight, assembled into war formation and came waddling out of the moonless dark, numbering nearly a thousand.

Grrff licked his lips, glancing at Silvermane.

"Well, big man, we had a pretty good run of luck, but let's not push our luck too far, eh? Time to get back, Grrff thinks!"

"I'm afraid you're right," admitted Silvermane. "But what about the Stone Man?"

Grrff threw one furry leg over Ishgadara's back, and climbed aboard. "He's probably still runnin'," said he nervously. "C'mon!"

"But we can't just go off and leave him."

"Why not? He's made of solid stone, ain't he? Them Ximchaks can't hurt him none, unless they got sledgehammers an' try to break him up for gravel. Let's get out of here before it's too late."

But it was already too late, for the long line of Ximchaks came at them, jabbing spears and letting fly a few feather-tufted arrows. Ganelon and Grrff looked at each other, then set their backs to the wall and unlimbered their weapons.

"Better get outa here, my girl," muttered Grrff to the Gynosphinx. "We got us a deal o' killing to do."

14.

Palensus Choy Remembers

They knew that by the time they could mount upon her back and the Gynosphinx could spread her wings and soar aloft, the Ximchak archers and spearmen could riddle Ishgadara through and through. So there was nothing to do but put their backs against the wall and stand and fight, hoping that Palensus Choy was aware of conditions beyond his walls, and would come to their aid with his sorcery before it was too late.

If it wasn't already too late, that is. The first few arrows were already shattering against the stone wall behind their backs, and Ganelon whipped out the Silver Sword to knock aside the first spear with the flat of the broad blade.

Grrff cursed under his breath in Tigermanic fashion, by his Claws and Whiskers, by his Teeth and Tail. They had been impossibly lucky to have fought off a hundred Ximchaks. Fighting off a thousand was much more impossible.

Oddly enough, it didn't prove necessary.

For, quite suddenly, the foremost ranks of the Barbarians froze in horror, petrified in their very tracks. Then a huge black shadow eclipsed the stars—unbelievably huge. And a breeze was blowing on them from a direction from which no breeze *could* blow—from behind their backs. Mystified, they glanced over their shoulders—

The castle was no longer there.

Then a shrill chorus of ululating horror broke from the lips of the astounded Ximchaks, and they stampeded in every direction, tossing aside their weapons in their haste to be gone from this haunted, unholy mountain.

The vast, angular black shadow blotted out the stars.

Grrff and Ganelon looked up.

Then they gasped, dropped their weapons, squeezed their eyes shut, and looked again. It was still there.

A weird bass-voiced chortling sound, like strangling bullfrogs at the bottom of a well, came to their ears. It was Ishgadara giggling.

"What's . . . so funny?" mumbled Grrff dazedly.

The sphinx-girl grinned.

"Master is rememberingk," she said.

"Remembering? Remembering *what?*"

"What him was forgettingk," she said. There was no need for her to explain it further, for the truth broke upon their minds in the same instant. No wonder the absent-minded magician had bemoaned his failure to recollect something of vital importance about Zaradon, something which would render unnecessary their attempts to defend the castle from its attackers.

Zaradon was a Flying Castle.

The Ximchaks got halfway back to the edge of the mountaintop before the Flying Castle drifted down and sat on them.

There were few left after that. When something like fifty thousand tons of masonry sits down on an army, not much of the army gets up and goes on afterward.

Zaradon had to sit down on the flat, plateaulike top of Naroob three times, however, before the Ximchaks were all squashed, since they had panicked off in all directions when the Flying Castle first took flight.

A thousand died there on the peak. The few who survived went over the edge and tried to get back down the sides of Mount Naroob as fast as they could, despite the fact that hundreds and hundreds and hundreds of slower-climbing Ximchaks were in their way, still grimly struggling up the face of the sheer cliff.

Quite a few fell, dislodging very many more. By then, of course, enough of the still-climbing Ximchaks had caught a glimpse of the Flying Castle and had decided to turn around and go back down. So precipitous were they in their quick decision that more than a few jumped and many others just plain fell. The rest discovered that however hard it had been for them to climb up Mount Naroob in the first place, it was a lot harder to climb down it. Especially at night. Very especially on a *moonless* night.

By this time, Ganelon and Grrff had found Chongrilar,

gotten back astride Ishgadara, and had caught up to Zaradon during its sit-downs on the Ximchak army. Ollub Vetch had finished making enough of the explosive to stuff into small jars, pots, and other receptacles. Armed with these makeshift bombs, the two warriors got back on Ishgadara and flew off to speed the Ximchaks down the sides of the mountain with a well-placed grenade or two. They found the explosive remarkably effective, and soon learned the knack of placing the bombs *just so,* in order to cause landslides. One of these landslides was so successful that it carried thirteen hundred Ximchaks to the base of the cliff in a rush, burying them under many tons of broken rock.

By morning, almost all of the Ximchaks had gotten down to the ground—one way or another—and the remnant which was still alive was to be counted in the dozens, if that. They headed through the mountains toward Gompland, and Grrff and Ganelon sped them on their way with the last of the grenades, before flying back to Zaradon for a much-overdue supper and a much-needed sleep.

The Battle of Mount Naroob was thus concluded in a manner enormously satisfactory to everyone involved in it except, of course, for those who were on the losing side—in this case, the Ximchaks.

But that's usually true of any battle.

They slept most of the next day away, rising about the fourth hour after midday to find an enormous breakfast hot and steaming and all ready for them, by courtesy of Chongrilar, who, being a magically animated statue of carven stone, never got tired and never needed to sleep, which made him in many ways an ideal servant.

After putting away as much of the meal as they could possibly stuff inside them, the victors lazily discussed what next to do. It seemed highly unlikely that the Ximchaks would accept this second defeat, having already demonstrated their unwillingness to swallow their first. On the other hand, there didn't seem to be much the Barbarians could do to fight against a Flying Castle, even if they wanted to.

"That's one of the nice things about Flying Castles, you know," murmured Palensus Choy offhandedly. "Not only are they proof against theft and burglary, to say the least, but siege and attack, to boot. If only I had been able to recall the fact that Zaradon was a Flying Castle, we should all have been spared so much worry and work and warring!"

Ollub Vetch, somewhat miffed that the saving of Zaradon had been accomplished by the sorcery of Palensus Choy, instead of by his own scientific labors in fabricating the explosives, sniffed disdainfully.

"Fancy forgettin' anything so important as the fact that your castle be actually an aerial contrivance!" he remarked spitefully.

Palensus Choy sighed. "Oh, dear me, you're right, of course—quite right! It's my immortality was to fault, you know, my dear chap. Living for six or so million years, you know, well, you accumulate an awful lot of things to remember. Only human of me to forget some of them, I expect. . . ."

Ollub Vetch snorted eloquently, but made no further rejoinder.

" 'Zactly how do Zaradon fly, anyway, master?" inquired Kurdi, who had been wriggling impatiently throughout the grownups' conversation, eager to get the question in.

"*Exactly*," said Ganelon.

"How *does*," said Grrff.

"Well, child," blinked the Immortal of Zaradon musingly, "that was part of what I had forgotten; so I had to, you know, look it up. Used to keep records, you know. Well. Anyway: the stone whereof the masonry of Castle Zaradon is composed was constructed is a quartzine synthetic, permeated with granules of *glegium*."

"*Glegium?*"

"Yes, *glegium*. You know: one of the so-called sentient metals, according to young Cardoxicus' intriguing theory . . ."

In his rambling and pedantic manner, Choy explained about this particular hypothesis, which extended evolutionary theory to the inclusion of even inanimate minerals, arguing that every form of matter in the universe was tending toward something very much like life, and even intelligence. *Glegium* lived, in a fashion, and was even self-aware to some dim degree. Since in nature it was found only in the cores of stars, it was vaguely cognizant of the fact that it didn't belong on Old Earth but up in the sky somewhere, and tried continuously to get back, fighting gravity when permitted to do so. Palensus Choy had permitted it to do so, hence the castle could fly.

"But that's *scientific*, 'pon my specific gravity, not your usual mystical mumbo-jumbo!" burst Vetch. And he was quite right, too; *glegium* was Element 121 on the Periodic Table, and the known isotope with the longest reported half-life has an atomic weight of 272.

Palensus Choy looked distressed and bit his lip.

"Hem. *Hrrmph!* Actually, you're quite right, my dear chap," he said feebly.

The fat inventor smirked triumphantly, but forebore to rub it in.

The others made little of this, but Ganelon had heard of *dianium,* at least, and knew something of these sentient metals. He was aware of the curiously antigravitic properties of *dianium,* for Istrobian's flying kayak utilized the self-same rare, ultratelluric mineral in achieving its own condition of weightlessness. The kayak, as my reader may remember, had been borrowed by Prince Erigon from the museum of Valardus and figured in one of Silvermane's more recent adventures.*

"I wonder if that's how Istrobian got his?" mused Ganelon to himself.

"Pardon?" inquired Palensus Choy politely.

Ganelon explained about the flying kayak. Choy remembered the magus in question, having briefly known him, and murmured something about his belief that Istrobian had synthesized the crystalline mineral by alchemical processes.

"But, my dear boy, how is it that you are acquainted with the works of the estimable Istrobian?" he asked. "Pardon me for saying so, but you are surely too young to have had your origin in that remote era."

Ganelon explained that his master, the famous Illusionist of Nerelon, had told him about Istrobian and the other leading thaumaturgists of the Epoch of the High Wizards.

"Nerelon? Nerelon? Don't seem to recall the fellow—was he around in those days?" murmured Choy. Ganelon answered that he really didn't know; he was much to polite to express his incredulity over the fact that Palensus Choy seemed not even to have heard of his master, whom he loyally considered the most famous of magicians then incarnate an old Earth.†

---

*I refer the interested reader to *The Enchantress of World's End.*

†Norovus, the author of the erudite Thirtieth Commentary on the Epic, inserts at this point a gloss to suggest that the Illusionist

Grrff was, by this time, yawning openly, revealing gleaming ivory fangs set in glistening black gums, and a prodigious tongue of a lovely shade of pink.

Not long thereafter he suggested that the hour was late and fighting one hundred Ximchaks had been a not unfatiguing day's work, and that he required more than just one night's sleep to recover therefrom. So they all went trooping off to bed, and Ganelon had to carry little Kurdi, who had dozed off already.

It had been a long day for them all.

But not so long as the days that were yet to come.

---

was known by some other cognomen during the Epoch. But Norovus was notoriously overclever and hair-splitting in his methods of argumentation: personally, I incline to the simpler, more insightful opinion of Argossa, in whose First Commentary it is suggested that even in those days Palensus Choy was singularly absent-minded and forgetful.

Book Three

THE MAD EMPIRE OF TRANCORE

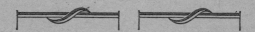

The Scene: The Mountains of Iriboth; Kuruz; Tabernoy; the Singing River; Island Trancore in the Greater Pommernarain Sea.

New Characters: Jrngka the Mantichore; the Piast Orillibus; the Gray Dynasts; the Emperor Scaviolis; madmen and other Trancorians; Wolf Turgo of the Ximchaks.

15.

Seven Strange Old Men

Bright and early the next morning the little gypsy boy woke up and slid out of bed. Ganelon Silvermane was still asleep, so Kurdi tried not to make any noise while bathing and getting dressed, in order not to awaken him.

Bathing—which Kurdi had become whole-heartedly converted to, such were the luxurious appointments of Castle Zaradon—was no problem, since with the door closed the blissful boy could splash and play in the warm tubful of pink and perfumed suds to his heart's content. Nor was dressing likely to disturb the slumbering giant, since dressing, for Kurdi, consisted of wriggling into a brief loincloth and poking his brown toes into small gilt slippers.

Once out the door, the lad scampered down to the kitchens, where Chongrilar had already prepared for him a hot, delicious breakfast of buttered pancakes drenched in purple syrup, a bowl of fresh guckleberries in cold milk, a mug of steaming hot cider, and three strips of succulent bacon, fried crisp and crunchy, just the way he liked them. The Stone Man watched as the boy gobbled down this repast, kicking his heels and talking all the while, and the normally gloomy and morose expression on the classically sculptured features of Chongrilar softened as he watched the child eat. Like all of the others in Castle Zaradon, the statue found the bright, good-natured, cheerful little boy irresistibly likable, and even his stony heart had by now developed a paternal fondness or avuncular affection for Ganelon's little squire.

After his breakfast, since none of the others were yet up, Kurdi repaired to the menagerie, where he had made friends with all of the mythological creatures who lived therein, even the Mantichore, Jrngka, who was rather grouchy and

ill-tempered, since this was his molting season. But his particular chum was Ishgadara, with whom he loved to talk
while combing her curly mane and grooming her tawny-
furred back and shoulders.

"Here he be agin, th' wee scamp," grumbled Jrngka with
pretended grumpiness. "None o' yer high jinks in here,
youngun! Pore ol' Rilly, she be tryin' t' catch a few months'
nap, and as fer me, wellsir, I hain't in no mood fer yer
scamperin' around and noise."

Kurdi paid no attention at all to this but hopped into the
Mantichore's stall and threw his brown arms around the old
creature's neck and gave him a good-morning hug, which
Jrngka pretended not to enjoy. The Mantichore resembled a
large crimson-furred lion with a bearded human face and
a wide mouth set with huge square teeth, two of which were
bright with gold fillings. He looked somewhat mangy and his
ribs poked out in a bony fashion, and he was losing his red
fur by the handful, since his winter coat was growing in.

"Git along wif ye now, scat!" said the grouchy old Mantichore fondly. Kurdi kissed him on his wet black nose and
went to the big water tank to peer in at the enormous, pale
length of the Piast, Orillibus, but she was still dozing through
the last weeks of her bicentennial hibernation period. With
her milky, pallid, partly translucent snaky length, begemmed
with tiny glinting scales like flakes of mica, the luminous, bejeweled tendrils which formed her skull crest, and her
enormous, serene, gentle eyes like great lambent pink opals,
he thought her the most beautiful creature he had ever seen;
and so she was. The pink eyes, half open, were dim with
dreams of a beautiful strangeness beyond conjecture. How he
wished she would awaken from her slumbers, so he could
love her as he loved the other weird and marvelous inhabitants of the private zoo of Palensus Choy!

Ishgadara was his favorite, and the boy liked nothing
more than to snuggle down beside her warm, furry, breathing hugeness and ask her questions. She mothered the child
in her comical, wise, big-hearted way, and told him stories
drawn from the immemorial sphinx-lore of her race, which
is part of the racial memory of her kind. She knew many
sphinxish legends and myths—how the first of her kind,
Chorondzon, had flown down from the Lost Moon before
the First Ice Age, when Atlantis was but the youngest child
of Mu the Motherland; how Jaspodnar the Sphinx-King had
led his people out of their bondage to the Black Warlocks

in the days before the Great Wall of China was built; how the Sphinx, the Lamia, and Darunzadar the Lamussa had ruled the Kingdom of the Dawn before the birth of Prester John. Oh, she knew many tales, and all of them were wonderful, and some of them were even true.

This morning Ishgadara sensed deep in her bones the slow approach of winter, a season which she loathed like all her mighty kind, who are native to the desert regions of the south, where winter never comes. So after greeting the boy and giving him a motherly snuzzle, she suggested they go and play in the garden, where a dome of clear crystal caught and focused the rays of the Sun like a great lens, making tropic warmth on this bleak, cold, windswept mountain peak. Kurdi readily agreed, for the gardens of Zaradon were as wonderous as almost everything else in the Flying Castle of Palensus Choy.

He liked the strange Moontree, with its slim black trunk and snakelike, slender boughs, which bore up discoid yellow leaves. The seed from which that tree had grown had been found on the Ninth Moon of Saturn and had been a birthday present to Palensus Choy from the crystalloid intelligence which ruled that frozen realm. Then there were the Singing Roses, stirring over to unfelt breezes, their vibrant corolla of pollen-dusted tendrils humming a sweet, atonal song to lure down the gorgeous, tapestry-winged moths which filled the dreamy air of Choy's enchanted garden with a beauty like unto flying flowers.

Sprawled out atop her broad back, on his tummy with his face buried in her warm and fragrant mane, the boy let his sphinxish friend wander where she wished, listening to her comfortable, deep-chested voice while she told him about the Great Migration at the end of the Golden Age, when the Grandfather of All Dragons made truce with the Elvish Kings, who opened the portals to the Halfworld of Faërie and let all of the mythological beings enter into their realm, which was beyond all time, as it was beyond all space, and where there was neither change nor death and pain and sadness could never come.

It was a beautiful story. And a true one, too.

Suddenly, she stopped short, jarring him awake from his lazy half-doze.

"Ishy? Wha's wrong?" the boy murmured, rubbing his eyes and looking around. Then he saw that which the wide emerald eyes of the sphinx-girl had seen, and he gasped with surprise.

The crystal dome which protected the enchanted garden from the wintry winds also, of course, magnified the view. And, staring down from their height (for the garden was a rooftop garden, and built atop the fourth tier of the Flying Castle), the two of them could clearly see a strange and curious procession which approached Zaradon through the clouds.

Kurdi blinked, squeezed his eyes shut, rubbed them with his knuckles, and looked again, but it was still there.

Sailing through the scudding clouds, directly for the top of Mount Naroob, floated something like a great ship with a high poop, ornately carven, ornamented with enormous flashing gems, brave with gold. Now Kurdi had never before seen a ship, a real ship, for that part of Gondwane the Great wherethrough his people, the Iomagoths, were wont to wander lies many hundreds of leagues from even the nearer of the Seven Inland Seas of the Supercontinent. But he had seen pictures of them, and knew what they should look like.

But this strange argosy of the skies had neither masts nor sails, keel nor rudder, and it was not fashioned out of wood, but from something which looked like glass. Upcurving high at prow and poop, it was shaped like the crescent moon, although fatter; and the glass of it was opalescent with colors, like a soap bubble blown by a giant.

In a row on the deck stood seven old men, robed in black, with tall tiaras glittering on their bald and wrinkled brows, and identical long beards of snowy white adangle on their chests. Their hands were clasped before them in a manner which was supplicational, and their eyes were closed as though in sleep.

"What *are* they, Ishy?" the boy breathed, wonderingly. "What do hit *mean?*"

"*Does* it mean," rumbled Ishgadara, her green eyes watchful and wary. "Me no knowingk. Quick—go tell master!"

In the great hall Palensus Choy held audience with the delegation from Trancore which had come to implore his sorcerous aid against the Ximchaks, who had made a thrust into their maritime realm. The seven old men were known as the Gray Dynasts, and they were, in effect, the rulers of Trancore. That was not literally true, of course, because nothing the Trancorians said was ever exactly or even quite true. The Emperor of the Trancorians, Scaviolis XII, actually ruled. But he was even madder than the other folk of Trancore, which was probably why the Habruztish Sibyl had named him Emperor in the first place.

They were all mad in Trancore. That's why it was called the Mad Empire.

These things Palensus Choy explained in his confused and absent-minded way to his friends, after the audience was adjourned and the seven Dynasts went into trance state while their host considered this application for help.

Grrff didn't understand anything of this, and said so in his gruff manner. Patiently, Choy tried to explain.

"The poor Trancorians are descended from the Cru Thoy Savants," he murmured. "The Savants devoted their entire energy to attempting the solution of the Safetilian Dilemma, which was actually impossible for a merely human intelligence to solve. It consumed their race with frustration and drove them all mad. This was long, very long, before the arrival of the Ninth Magistrate, of course."

"The who?"

"The one who solved the Dilemma."

"Oh. So?"

"Their madness proved inheritable, and the Empire of their descendants has been a Mad Empire ever since."

"And we're going to go and help them? A nation of crazy people?"

"That's what I must decide," groaned Palensus Choy, wearily. "All this worry and confusion, and all because of those unmannerly ruffians! When will things ever return to normal, so that I may get back to my work again?"

"How does their ship fly?" asked Silvermane sensibly. "Is it *dianium* or *glegium* or something?"

"Oh, it doesn't fly, my dear boy; ships cannot fly," muttered Palensus Choy abstractedly.

"Then how did the seven old geezers *get* here?" demanded the Tigerman, beginning to lose his temper at all this mystifying stuff.

"They didn't. They aren't here at all," mumbled Choy, plucking at his beard.

"Where-at is this-here place, Trancore, anyway?" piped up little Kurdi. For once, Grrff and Ganelon were too distracted with their own confused thoughts to correct his bad English. (I mean *Gondwanish*.)

"I'm sure I don't know," said Choy in his maddening way. "I'm sure it must be around someplace. . . ."

Grrff threw up his hands, or rather his paws, giving up in disgust.

"Grrff gives up," he announced. "Has th' whole world gone crazy?"

"No, of course not. Only Trancore. And that was ten million years ago, give or take . . ."

His voice trailed off as Grrff uttered a snort which shook the candlesticks, and stalked off out of the hall in disgust.

16.

Prince Erigon Invites

While the others were having an early lunch that same day, Palensus Choy busied himself in his librarium, from which he eventually emerged to report success in researching the whereabouts of the Mad Empire of Trancore.

"The geographer Xorex seems never to have heard of the place, and Quilian is of the erroneous opinion that it lies way down south of the Smoking Mountains, this side of Chuu," he explained in his meandering, loquacious way. "On the other hand, Selestor, whose geographical writings I have always considered accurate and highly authentic insofar as Greater Zuavia, Lesser Zuavia, and those portions of Northern YamaYamaLand which border on, ah, ahem!, the border are concerned believes—"

"Oh, get to the point, can't you?" huffed Ollub Vetch around a cheekful of marinated cheese sandwich.

"Heh? Hum. Well, then: a considerable distance to the north-northwest, beyond the Iribôth Mountains, beyond Kuruz and Tabernoy, on the other side of the Singing River. It is built on three islands in the midst of the Greater Pommernarian Sea, and borders upon the northwestern parts of the country of the Gomps, due west of the Thunder Troll Mountain."

They digested that body of information, and their luncheon, at the same time.

"Why did these nutty old geezers come to you with their problems, anyway?" inquired Grrff, bluntly.

"Probably because, if I may say so, I am the most powerful magician in Greater Zuavia, known, if I may also say so, for my benign and protective interest in the security of those nations which are my neighbors," said Choy complacently.

Grrff pricked up his ears, his furry features reflecting a certain skepticism.

"Why didn't you help the Gomps when they were invaded by the Ximchaks, then?" he demanded.

"That is a reasonable question, my furry friend. Alas, ahem, my attentions were engaged elsewhere at the time, and word did not reach me of the danger of the Thirty Cities until the Gompish Regime had already been extirpated. Dear me, if only the poor Gomps had been as foresighted as the Mad Trancorians, and had requested my assistance in repelling the Ximchak invasion, none of these recent events would have happened at all, and Gondwane would have been spared much suffering and slaughter!"

"Speaking of the Trancorians," interrupted Ganelon, "you were saying just this morning that the seven old men didn't really fly here in their glass boat. Do you mind explaining what you meant by that?"

"Of course, my dear boy, only too happy. I meant exactly what I said. The celestial vessel, together with its occupants, is a thought projection and nothing more. A mentally induced illusion."

"An illusion?" demanded Ollub Vetch incredulously. "How can that be—telepathy, you mean? Hoy! I thought these Trancorians were all nutty—"

"They are," Palensus Choy nodded affably. "In the case of the Gray Dynasts, their madness consists in the firm belief that they possess a degree of sagacity bordering upon omniscience, with some of the related powers omniscience is popularly supposed to have access to. The convictions of insanity often produce phenomena remarkably verifying the delusions of that insanity. Thus, at least, concludes the philosopher Camballio; Llambichus, on the contrary, points out—"

"Anoth-err aer-rial ve-hic-cle app-rroaches," boomed the Stone Man's stentorian voice from the battlements of the first tier. They went to the nearest window, which was up on the balcony which ran around the hall at the level of the second story, and peered in the direction from which Chongrilar gloomily announced their visitors to be nearing. It was the flying kayak from Valardus, with Prince Erigon and the Sirix Xarda of Jemmerdy seated therein.

Chongrilar waved them down to a landing on the flat surface of the tier, and helped anchor the weightless conveyance to one of the waterspouts. The two young people dismounted and entered, to greet their friends.

"My royal father wishes me to invite you all back to Valardus for certain festivities," explained Prince Erigon after the exchange of greetings was accomplished.

"Indeed!" murmured Palensus Choy, with polite interest. "And may I inquire as to the nature of these festivities?"

"They are those attendant upon a royal wedding," explained the Prince of Valardus pridefully. Xarda blushed crimson, which shade clashed abominably with her red hair, but looked starry-eyed with happiness. They crowded around, burbling congratulations, and Ganelon shook hands with the Valardine heir, then gravely saluted the girl knight of Jemmerdy with a solemn kiss on the cheek, which was most unusual for him. She kissed him back and gave him a little hug, which was even more unusual for her.

"I am delighted to hear of your impending nuptials," stated Palensus Choy, "but very much fear certain pressing and urgent matters to the north and northwest will render my attendance upon your festivities improbable." In his usual wandering and verbose manner he explained something of what had been going on in the eight days since they had flown hither from Valardus.

"Four against one hundred!" breathed Xarda, eyes shining. Her chivalric instincts were aroused by such odds. "Zounds! Would that I had been able to stand with you, to measure my steel against the varlets!"

They repaired to the hall below, and Chongrilar broached a flagon of excellent vintage, whereupon they toasted the happy pair, and wished them an abundance of joy commensurate to their deserving.

"I take it, then," puffed Ollub Vetch, "that you do intend going off to Trancore in answer to they request for help against the Ximchaks?"

Palensus Choy toyed with his beard, eyes serious. "Well, my dear Vetch, I was contemplating some sort of aerial reconnaissance of Gompland anyway, curious to see how the remaining Ximchaks and this ferocious Warlord of theirs were taking their defeats at Valardus and Zaradon. So I might as well look in at Trancore and see what is eventuating there. . . ."

"Good," nodded Ganelon Silvermane thoughtfully. "I was hoping you felt that way, Master Choy, and even if you weren't so inclined, I had just about decided to ask you to let me and Grrff borrow Ishgadara for just such a trip of our own. Now I expect you will be taking the Flying Castle, though?"

The Immortal shuddered fastidiously and closed his eyes in abhorrence.

"I should say not!" he exclaimed. "You should see the damage our last flight, however brief, inflicted upon the kitchen crockery! To say nothing of my vases, bric-a-brac, and the glassware in my laboratorium! No, no, my dear boy —a thousand times, *no*. Ishgadara shall carry you and me and our dear friend from Karjixia, and my colleague Vetch, if he cares to join the expedition—"

"Hoy! Not *me*, if you don't mind," puffed the fat inventor, shaking his head vigorously. "I've had quite enough activity to last me for a while, thank you very much! Besides, I must get me notes in shape on the chemical experiments which led to my perfection of the explosive substance, while everything is still clear in mind. Then there be a few further experiments I would like to conduct, to see if the substance can be further refined and improved—"

"Very well," said Palensus Choy wearily. "But *do* be careful about causing any more of those dreadful explosions, won't you, my dear chap? I shall give instructions to Chongrilar that you will remain in charge here while the rest of us are looking into things up north."

"Sure," agreed Ollub Vetch with a mischievous grin. "And explain to me before you go how your vision-crystal works, eh? That way I can look in on you from time to time, and see how you do be gettin' along. That way, if you get into some trouble that your magical mumbo-jumbo can't get you out of, mayhap old Ollub Vetch can lend you a hand with a little of his trusty science to the rescue!"

Palensus Choy pinched his thin lips together, the glint of argumentation appearing in his vague old eyes, and Silvermane hastily interrupted with a question about the flight in order to stave off yet another exchange of insults in the interminable verbal duel between the exponents of science versus sorcery.

Bidding their friends a reluctant and lingering farewell, Prince Erigon and the former girl knight of Jemmerdy, soon to become his Princess, returned to Istrobian's flying kayak and flew back to Valardus, wishing the adventurers all good luck and success on their mission to the north.

Palensus Choy informed the Gray Dynasts of his decision

to visit Island Trancore amidst the Greater Pommernarian Sea, and the seven solemn sages departed in their imaginary glass sky-boat to convey his promise to their Emperor.

Kurdi pled and begged and bothered them for permission to go along on the trip, and Ganelon reluctantly gave his approval. As he explained things to Grrff the Xombolian later on that afternoon, there was no valid reason to deny the boy his wishes, since they were only going to fly around and investigate the Ximchak activities from the air, and Kurdi would be perfectly safe with them.

Grrff, who came from a warrior race where even youngsters received plenty of training in warfare, plus some solid experience, thought it was a good idea.

They departed from Zaradon late that afternoon, Choy, Kurdi, Grrff, and Ganelon, mounted on the back of the sphinx-girl. For this particular expedition they brought along a picnic basket of provisions, packed away in saddlebags slung over the haunches of Ishgadara, since they would certainly be absent from Zaradon overnight. Choy packed away Selestor's map of the region, and some magical equipment of his own which he thought might come in handy if they *did* run into any trouble.

"After all, since we were active in, ah, discouraging the Ximchaks both at Zaradon and Valardus, they are not likely to feel particularly friendly to us, you know," murmured the old magician absently.

Grrff uttered a snarling laugh. "Ol' Grrff *does* admire yer gift for understatement, old man! 'Tween what happened at Valardus and what happened atop Mount Naroob, them Barbarians lost about eight thousand fightin'-men. *'Discouraged,'* indeed! Hoppin' mad, is more like it!"

There was an ominous ring of truth to his prediction which none of them liked very much. They took to the air.

17.

The Singing River

North of Mount Naroob the Iriboth Mountains rose in a titanic wall, through which they passed by means of a cleft in the peak of one mountain, whose cloven crest reminded Ganelon Silvermane of Mount Luz, the twin-pinnacled mountain where the Death Dwarves had set an ambush to capture him and the Illusionist in the Bazonga bird.* This time, happily, there was no ambush.

Beyond the great range of mountains, where the crust of Old Earth had buckled into an enormous ridge higher than the Legendary Himalayas, from the inexorable pressure created millions of years ago when the planet's floating continents had been driven together to form the colossal landmass called Gondwane, lay wrinkled hills with verdant valleys set between them. And beyond these, small kingdoms and city-states appeared upon the landscape.

They flew over Kuruz first: Kuruz, with its lapis spires and walls of gleaming turquoise, where men wear veils of mauve gauze and women wear nothing at all, save for a few strategically situated opals. Kuruz was the most inhospitable of all the cities of Greater Zuavia, and the very existence of non-Kuruzites was not tolerated therein. The reason for this, as Palensus Choy explained, was that the laws whereby the folk of Kuruz were governed, even though they had been handed down by the Gods through their Prophet, Ku, were extremely foolish and silly laws, and strangers were more than likely to laugh at them.

Well did the Kuruzites know that their laws were stupid

*See Chapters 15-16 of my redaction of the First Book of the Epic, *The Warrior of World's End.*

and frivolous; still, they *were* the laws of Kuruz, and not to be the occasion of ridicule by mere strangers. Hence no strangers were permitted within Kuruz for any reason whatsoever; such as the civic pride of the Kuruzites, even in their own foolish laws.

North of Kuruz the land flattened out into a vast level plain dotted with shallow lakes. They flew, just before sunset, across the hugest of these, which was almost but not quite large enough to qualify as one of the seven inland seas of Gondwane the Great. It was indeed known to the Zuavians as the Lesser Pommernarian Sea, although its breadth was not, to be honest, sufficient to earn it that name. It had been discovered by one Agzan of Pommernar ages before, in the course of his leadership of the Pommernarian Migration commanded by Iksk, God of Revelations. This equivocal divinity had instructed his servant, Agzan, that the Promised Land of the Pommernarians lay between two mighty seas, the larger of which was situated to the north of the Blessed Country, and the smaller to the south. Since the Pommernarians had then been wandering about Gondwane for the better part of six hundred years and were getting pretty fed up with this sort of thing, Agzan seized the opportunity afforded by the positioning of the large sea just north of the medium-sized lake, declared the lake to be the Lesser Pommernarian Sea by his direct, personal fiat, and instructed his foot-weary and short-tempered people to settle into their Promised Land.

The Gods, however, are not wisely mocked, even one as insignificant as Iksk, who seldom deserved more than a footnote or two in the more respectable of mythologies. First the Pommernarians suffered a plague of toads, followed by a plague of sleepwalking, and then a widespread attack of the seven-year itch. Eventually, deciding their prophet had only told them what they wanted to hear, which is not always the same thing as the truth, they rose up, stoned the unfortunate Agzan, and wandered off into the east, where they vanished from the knowledge of men, still, it was presumed, searching for the Promised Land.

The names, however, had stuck, and to this day the former lake was still known as the Lesser Pommernarian Sea, even though it was only a quarter of a mile across.

On the northern shore of the sea there rose a dilapidated and mangy-looking huddle of ramshackle huts known as Tabernoy, City of Atheists, where still dwelt the disillusioned

descendants of those few of the Pommernarian Migrants who
had lost their faith in Iksk because of the ineptitude of his
prophet, Agzan. Their descendants were still adherent of the
atheistical doctrines of Tabernus the Dissenter to this day.
Tabernus, formerly the chief disciple of Agzan, had lost his
enthusiasm for religion when he narrowly escaped stoning
alongside the unlucky Agzan, he being lucky enough to fall
foaming in an eipleptic fit. Since the Pommernarians super-
stitiously venerated epileptics, considering all demented per-
sons to have been touched by the Gods, his infirmity led to
his survival during the insurrection. The ingrate Tabernus,
however, lost all faith in divinity as a profession, preached
atheism as the only doctrine suitable to intelligent beings,
gathered about him a ragtag following, and settled down in a
slovenly community on the north shore, rather than go wandering off with the others in search of a will-of-the-wisp.

They flew offer Tabernoy, which was even less appetizing
from the ground than it seemed from aloft, and continued
their progress into the northwest.

They were flying along the borders of Gompish territory
now, and saw in the distance the blackened rubble of twelve
or thirteen of the Thirty Cities once dominated by the now-
extirpated Regime. The Ximchaks, it seemed, from the sorry
condition of these sooty ruins, had a dislike of cities.

Night fell while they were still skirting the edges of Gompland, and they were getting about as sleepy as Ishgadara was
getting tired, so they decided to land and spend the night
on the ground.

They built a fire, Kurdi gathering driftwood from the
the shores of a nearby river, and Palensus Choy touching
it alight with his enchanter's wand. This was a rod of behe-
moth-ivory carvan into the likeness of a winged and ser-
pent-wreathed caduceus.

Feasting on the contents of the well-stuffed picnic basket
which Chongrilar had prepared, they basked drowsily in the
warmth of the fire, chatting lazily for a time, then one by one
rolling up in cloak, blanket or sleeping bag, and drifting into
sleep.

Grrff was awakened by the most horrendous screeching
cry that had ever assaulted his long and furry ears. Blinking
the sleepiness from his eyes, the Tigerman sprang out of his
bedroll, clutching around him frantically to find his ygdraxel,

which he had put down somewhere beside him before retiring.*

Locating his weapon and snatching it up, the Xombolian came to his feet, staring around in the darkness to discover the source of that hideous screech, now dying away in long-drawn-out sobbing ululations.

Ganelon had been awakened by the cry as well; stark naked, clutching the pommel of the Silver Sword, the bronze giant glared about him in a manner similar to Grrff's.

As for little Kurdi, who had been sharing the cozy warmth of Silvermane's cloak, the boy remained exactly where he was, although wide awake. He had pulled the cloak up over his head so that only his eyes were visible. Wide and frightened, they searched the gloom from side to side, while their owner tried frantically to recall the Iomagothic charms against night-wandering Grimps, Googs, and Gobblewopplies his old grandmother had taught him long ago.

Search as they might, the two warriors could discern nothing in the proximity of the camp. Grrff knelt to stir up the glowing coals of the fire and to feed it with some fresh wood while Ganelon went over to the tall yotzle tree in whose boughs Ishgadara had made her sleeping nest.

The sphinx-girl was sound asleep and snoring like a sawmill. Ganelon had to push and poke and prod her curled-up form in order to rouse her.

"No gettingk up yet, please," she mumbled sleepily. "Forty winks . . ."

When he finally managed to wake her up, she cocked her ears and searched the night with huge, moony eyes of lambent green. The sobbing ululation had died to an eerie groaning sigh, but erelong it started up, in a blood-curdling scream that went on and on for such a long time that no human lungs, and few belonging to even the bestial fauna of

*Glancing over the several preceding chapters, I notice that I have heretofore merely mentioned the ygdraxel by name without bothering to describe it. Suffice it to say, therefore, that the traditional Karjixian weapon resembles a long-handled billhook terminating in a tridentlike arrangement consisting of three hooked, razory, curved blades like cat's claws, the whole designed so that by manual adjustments the claw-hooks open and close. Quite obviously a mechanical equivalent of a tiger's claws, and therefore, considering the feline ancestry of the Tigermen, just the sort of weapon they might devise.

Gondwane, could possibly have held enough air to give voice to so interminable a cry.

"No seeingk nothingk," she said hoarsely. "Askingk master, big man!"

Now that it was brought to Silvermane's attention, it did seem odd to him that the night-howlings had aroused all of them except for the old Immortal, who was still sound asleep and snoring with a prolonged and nasal whistling sound. Ganelon went over and shook him awake, discovering that Palensus Choy had stuffed his ears with cotton batting before retiring.

"It's the Singing River, my boy, didn't I mention it earlier? Goodness me, how forgetful I am becoming! Well, ahem, the river flows very swiftly in these parts, and it is thickly grown with a variety of hollow reeds through which the current is forced, which drives out the air sharply. Such is the construction of the reeds, that the air makes a singing noise as it is forced through the reeds by the rushing water. Now go back to sleep, there's a good lad!"

" 'Singin' River, eh?" growled Grrff when Ganelon had returned with Choy's explanation to the mystery. " 'Blood-Curdling Howling River' 's what ol' Grrff'd call it. Gimme some o' that cotton, and let's hope this country doesn't have any more surprises up its sleeve for us, at least not till morning!"

18.

The City of Masks

By midmorning of the next day they were skirting the borders of the Gomp country, and from their height could see in the misty reaches of the far distance three of the Gompish cities. Choy identified them, from Selestor's map of this region, as Warwhith, Rosch, and Harbanay. Even from so great a remove it was obvious to the travelers that these towns lay in blackened ruins.

"Them Ximchaks," growled Grrff under his breath, his muzzle wrinkling. "When they get through talkin' a city, there ain't much of it left standing!"

Silvermane nodded grimly. They flew on. The Embosch Mountains formed the natural borders for the Gompish Regime, at least from south to north. Flying just beyond the mountains, they flew north, passing Rith River country and the Five Towns of Xarge, which formed a territory known as Ruggosh. Just over the mountains lay another Gompish metropolis, Embosch City; like the three other cities of the Regime they observed it to be a mound of sooty rubble.

"Wonder if *all* of the Thirty Cities are like this," mused the Tigerman rhetorically, not really wanting an answer.

The tallest peak in the northern parts of the Embosch range was called Thunder Troll Mountain. The Greater Pommernarian Sea lay due west of this immense mountain, with Island Trancore situated almost exactly in the center thereof. This sea was many times more vast than the Lesser Sea which they had flown over the previous evening; that had been little more than a lake, while this one must have measured hundreds of square miles.*

*During the age of Ganelon Silvermane (the Eon of the Falling Moon, it was called) there were seven inland seas upon the Super-

103

Directing Ishgadara to turn west as Thunder Troll Mountain loomed to their right, they soared across the Ovarva Plains, crossed the broad, sluggish floods of Wryneck River, and flew out over the sea. As they approached Trancore, their initial impression was that of a once-splendid metropolis now far gone into decay. They could see from their lofty vantage that the island had gradually submerged over the ages, for the extensive suburbs of the imperial capital trailed off down the sloping shores of Trancore, and extended underwater for a considerable distance. It was a trifle unnerving to see thoroughfares and rooftops underwater, and odd to see a few of the taller minarets, still standing after ages of neglect, thrusting their corroded and moldy spires above the waves.

"Ahem!" Palensus Choy, for all the world like a schoolmaster, cleared his throat for attention, continuing: "Trancore was once a city of perfectly enormous size, indeed, the largest in all of Gondwane at its peak. Gradually, however, a lake formed about the outer reaches, the water driven to the surface from underground springs, by enormous pressure; today, nearly five-eights of the metropolis has been submerged beneath the waves."

They descended toward a central structure called the Bryza, an acropolis hill crowned with hoary temples, crumbling fanes, and ruined shrines, and dominated by the hollow shell of a truly sumptuous palace complex, now in an advanced stage of decay, after uncounted centuries of complete neglect.

And as they came down upon the palace roof, a curious change seemed to take place. It was as if a film which had formerly obscured their vision was now whisked away, or as if an optical illusion, which had seemed real from one angle of vision, was now seen through from a different perspective. For what they had originally considered to be ruins, walls

---

continent of Gondwane. The Sea of Arbalon was the largest, Quadquoph the second largest, and Zelphodon the third. The Sea of Vlad and the sea called the Greater Pommernarian were of almost equal size and extent, but Vlad was judged to be the fourth and the Pommernarian the fifth. There was some confusion over the status of the Sea of Erium on the northern coast of the continent, some authorities considering it one of the Seven Inland Seas and others judging it to be a landlocked bay. The largest of all the inland seas was the Lost Sea of Voorm, which had dried up by the 250th Millennium of the Eon, and whose bed became the Voormish desert in Northern YamaYamaLand. It had been more than half again as big as Arbalon.

slumping into rubble, streets choked with refuse, towers tilted awry, could now be seen as being in perfect repair. In fact, the city sparkled in the sunlight—whole, immaculate, glorious.

"Is Grrff gone soft in the head, or bad in the eyes, or what?" muttered that worthy in *sotto voce* tones.

"Hush," cautioned Palensus Choy. "Here comes someone."

Through a crumbling portal, whose rotting masonry bore scabs of tarnished and peeling gilt, slouched three slack-jawed, lank-cheeked oafs with lackluster eyes, matted locks, and dirty hands, their skinny forms wrapped in greasy, tattered rags.

The visitors blinked, rubbed their eyes, looked again. Now through a gleaming archway, brave with gilt, strolled three graceful, nimble young heralds in gorgeous tabards stiff with embroidery.

These three smooth-cheeked, cherub-faced boys performed supple bows and led them into the interior of the palace. Cobwebs clung to rotting tapestries—a clutter of dusty furniture encumbered mildewed carpets. Then, in a twinkling, the chamber freshened, brightened, sparkled with gleaming ivory, amber, pearl inlay and waxed teak.

Muttering the names of several premier divinities from the Vemenoid Pantheon, the Zul-and-Rashemba Mythos, and High Quaxianity, the visitors steeled themselves, and went on.

An immense archway led into a huge, circular rotunda so vast in extent and so high-roofed as to seem a forum in the open air. The tiled floor was bestrewn with rotting garbage, fallen leaves, and mouldering fragments of masonry which had, over millennia, crumbled and become loosened, falling from the upper works.

Atop a cracked and muddy dais, a drooling, obese, half-naked cretin lolled, idly picking his nose while regarding them with dull, vacant eyes. Near the dais a huddle of decrepit old rheumy-eyed scarecrows crouched, mumbling bits of food between toothless jaws.

Again in the flicker of a lash, everything was transformed. The immense hall became spotless, magnificent, thronged with crowds of nobility in bejeweled raiment. Now enthroned on a winged chair of diorite, a majestic and imposing personage wrapped in robes of purple adorned with gold tassels lounged in kingly grandeur, and ranged about the foot of the dais stood the solemn and sagacious old gentlemen who had come to Zaradon in the flying glass boat to implore Choy's help.

"Witchcraft!" hissed little Kurdi, eyes gleaming bright with superstitious fear as he glanced around at the miraculously transformed throneroom.

"But that's impossible," breathed Palensus Choy faintly. "No one knows better than a magician when he is looking at an illusion, induced by an enchanter, or a glamour cast by a spell!"

"Then how you es'plain all this?" groaned Ishgadara, rolling her huge green eyes in alarm.

"I can't; I don't understand it; but please keep calm, all of you," whispered Palensus Choy. "Whatever the nature, cause, and purpose of the illusion, these people are friendly, hospitable, and mean us no harm."

Now an unctuous Chamberlain waddled forward, crowned with snowy plumes, bearing a huge silver mace-of-ceremony. He introduced himself as Lord Harpedon and conducted them forward to the foot of the dais, bowing with magnificent aplomb.

While Palensus Choy and the Emperor Scaviolis conversed in a florid exchange of elaborately polite but essentially meaningless and ritualistic compliments, Ganelon Silvermane, easily bored by the formalities of court, glanced around him interestedly. It was the boy Kurdi, however, whose bright, inquisitive eyes first spotted the Ximchak chieftain lounging on a marble bench across the hall, chewing on the rind of a juicy fruit and tossing scraps of its skin into the mouth of a large ornamental urn.

"Wha's *he* doin' here?" whispered the boy, tugging at Ganelon's arm, pointing urgently.

"What is," said Ganelon automatically. Then, seeing the Ximchak, he frowned. "I don't know; let's find out."

He caught Grrff's eye, called him over, and the two of them strolled across the rotunda, with Kurdi scampering excitedly in the rear. As they came up to where he was lazily lounging on the marble bench, the Ximchak looked up and saw them. The glint of humor appeared in his scarlet eyes.

"By Zaar, but you're the white-haired giant who cut out boys to ribbons on the mountaintop last week!" the Barbarian swore. Then he laughed. "What a fight that one was, or should I call it a fiasco? Poor Farrash will never live it down!"

"Who's he?" demanded Grrff, bluntly.

"The subchief in command of the first Hundred who

reached the peak," grinned the Ximchak wickedly. "The hulking lout let two warriors, a walking idol, and a winged lioness stomp his command into jelly. The Warlord nearly had him roasted alive for it, Farrash being unlucky enough to escape with a whole skin, as did I—"

"You were there on Naroob?" asked Silvermane somberly. The young savage nodded, grinning.

"I led the second Hundred over the top. Lucky for me the Warlord understands that when the foe have Flying Castles on their side, no commander has much of a chance. But you two fought one hell of a battle between you," he added admiringly.

Ganelon looked the young man over, and rather reluctantly the bronze giant liked what he saw. The Ximchak was about twenty, taller and straighter than most of his kind, with a gleaming chocolate-brown hide, half-naked under iron-gray furs and polished black leather harness and high-laced boots. His lean brown features were clean-cut, glowing with health, vibrant with virile energy, and even handsome in a wolfish way, despite the feral scarlet eyes. He had an air about him that was appealing, devil-may-care, laughing, rather mischievous. But he was a Ximchak. And Ganelon was here to fight Ximchaks.

"What's your name?"

"Turgo," said the other. "Wolf Turgo, they called me. And don't you or your furry friend get any ideas, big fellow: I'm a full chieftain of the Horde, here on embassy to His High-and-Mighty Nuttiness over there, who's gabbin' with your bearded friend. Flag o' truce, while we're on neutral ground?"

"Don't trust 'im," growled Grrff, fingering his ygdraxel and eyeing the young warrior with just that same hungry glint in his eye that his feline ancestors had in theirs whenever something that urgently needed killing came slithering through the underbrush.

"Are you here alone?" asked Ganelon.

Wolf Turgo shrugged carelessly. "Honor guard of five warriors, that's all."

"All right, then, flag of truce it is, Wolf Turgo," nodded Silvermane.

"Here comes the Grand Cockalorum of this madhouse," said the Ximchak, nodding to where the fat Chamberlain came waddling over with a stately and dignified old silver-haired gentleman in tow. "That's Lord Riolphus, the Seneschal," Wulf chuckled. "I call him th' High Panjandrum.

They're both as nutty as a goxxle tree in autumn—or haven't you seen through it all yet?"

"Seen through what?" asked Silvermane uncomfortably, remembering the curious illusion of decaying grandeur and toothless scarecrows among the mounded garbage.

Wolf Turgo grinned and winked.

"The Grand Cockalorum's going to invite you to a state banquet tonight. And th' High Panjandrum's going to escort you to what looks like a palatial suite. If you're still fooled by appearances by banquet hour tonight, big fellow, I'll tell you the whole trick. Oh, don't look so surprised: I'm invited to the banquet, too."

As the Seneschal, Riolphus, led them toward a grand marble staircase and up to their suite, Ganelon frowned in puzzlement. He was not baffled so much by what Wolf Turgo was doing here, as by his singular lack of resentment at being so soundly whipped.

And then there was the mystery of Trancore itself!

Already he found himself looking forward to the banquet hour, although he was not in the least hungry.

19.

Wolf Turgo Explains

For a palace of such grandeur of proportion and immensity of extent, it seemed remarkable to Ganelon Silvermane and his companions that there were not more servants to be seen.

"All that marble to polish, all those floors to sweep, all this bric-a-brac to dust," mused Palensus Choy baffledly. "We should be virtually falling over the help, every time we turn around! By the Purple Helix, this place is filled with mysteries!"

But it was true: not so much as a single servant was to be seen in the entirety of the palace and its labyrinthine congeries of hall and suites and staircases.

"Maype they clean-um wiv magic?" purred Ishgadara, rolling her eyes.

"Or invisible spirits, hey?" suggested Grrff the Xombolian, glancing about as if to catch off-guard legions of insubstantial genies.

"Stuff and nonsense!" sniffed the magician irritably. "I assure you again, my dear friends, that the use of thaumaturgy or the employment of elemental servitors could not possibly remain undetected by a sorcerer of my accomplishments. In the absence of our estimable colleague Ollub Vetch, who not being persent is thereby unable to disagree with me, let me say that my phloigms* are of unusual sensi-

---

*Phloigms are organs situated in the human forebrain which are sensitive to the presence of spiritual beings or the usage of occult, divine, supernatural, or magical forces. And incidentally, Palensus Choy is in error attributing the abnormal development of his phloigms to his excessive longevity. As the Ninth Commentary points out, the organs had already atrophied to a vestigial state by

tivity. I date, you will understand, from an era sufficiently remote in time that in the epochs of my youth the invaluable organs had not yet atrophied to a merely vestigial appendage, as is the case with you youngsters!"

"Well, then, Grrff gives up," grumbled that worthy. "For all we know, once a week, all the Trancorian grandees pitch in and have 'emselves a general clean-up day."

They whiled away the hours before the banquet, each in a different manner. Choy browsed through a vellum-bound copy of Phorospher's *Compendium Magicorum,* finally dozing off. Kurdi brushed and polished Silvermane's war harness and accouterments, and whetted the razory edges of the Silver Sword, then scampered off to play with Ishgadara in a rooftop garden adjoining their sumptuous suite. Ganelon and the Tigerman played *fexl,* an antique boardgame which employed a multiplicity of ivory pieces in simulated war.

When the ornate gold-and-crystal clepsydra on the jasper mantelpiece chimed the appointed hour, they all trooped down to the banqueting hall and found a long, high-ceilinged room whose walls were screens of fretted alabaster. There they reclined on cushion-strewn mats beside low tables heaped with succulent dishes. Wine goblets hollowed from enormous amethysts stood by each feasting place. Cautiously sipping his, Palensus Choy found to his pleasure that the beverage was rare Ahhorian of a pricely vintage.

Unseen musicians, presumably stationed behind the alabaster wall-screens, played a peculiar atonal but not displeasing music to accompany the meal. The instruments sounded like none of those with which Ganelon Silvermane was acquainted; and the style of the compositions was likewise unfamiliar to him, being in the most antique Zuavian modes.

Wolf Turgo came slouching in when the banquet was well commenced. Disregarding the obvious wishes of the Grand Cockalorum, Harpedon, who attempted to lead him to a seat on the other side of the hall, the Ximchak sat down at Ganelon's table, grinning impudently in the direction of the

---

the Eon of the Thought Magicians, two hundred million years before this time, and Palensus Choy, although of a remarkable age, six and one-half million years, was certainly not *that* old. The Commentary provides what is probably the most accurate explanation for Choy's anomaly: that the practice of any of the Sixty Sciences stimulates the phloigmal health of the individual.

annoyed dignitary. He looked the platters over with a tolerant grimace, his eyes sly and mocking.

"Enjoying that muck, are you?" he asked Silvermane.

The bronze giant, surprised, was about to mouth some polite phrase when he paused to reconsider. No gourmandizer, Ganelon seldom noticed what he was eating, and was indifferent to the whole art of cuisine, hardly knowing the flavor of one spice or sauce from another. He had always considered the enthusiasms of the gourmet too effete for him. But now that the young Ximchak called his attention to the matter, he could not help but observe that the food he had been stuffing himself with, although luscious to the eye, was somewhat rancid to the palate, where it was not actually flavorless, and flavorless where it was not slightly rancid.

He turned to see if his friends seemed to have noticed any similar experience, but found them crunching and munching away, listening to the dreamy strains of music.

Wolf Turgo grinned sardonically.

"Still haven't figured it out, have you?"

"Figured *what* out?" asked Silvermane.

"The mystery of Trancore," said the Barbarian. "Where things are never what they *seem* to be, and what they *seem* to be is not what they really *are.*"

"If you are being enigmatic merely to impress us, you young ruffian, kindly desist," murmured Palensus Choy with asperity. "But if you know something valuable or important, please speak plainly and to the point. It is considered a breach of manners, among the imperial Zuavians, to converse while ingesting nutriment."

Turgo made a wry face at these fancy words.

"*You're* the wizard, old fellow," he said. "Got a talisman or amulet of Ukwukluk about you, perchance?"

Choy blinked uncertainly. The divinity in question was a godling of the Vemenoid Pantheon known as the Dispeller of Delusions. In that particular mythology he was generally depicted as in conflict with Nerelus the Shadowmaker, a deity borrowed from the Polydeuxianity by way of the Horxite heresy.

"Why, actuallly, I believe I do," murmured Choy distractedly. He removed the supple silkskin pouch from his girdle and dug through the collection of periapts, amulets, eidolons, and talismanic rings which the pouch contained. Therefrom he at length selected a small oval scarab of blue paste cut with the cartouche of Ukwukluk, and turned it absently between his fingers, studying the magical characters graven in the obverse side.

Silvermane noticed that the hue of the scarab was the precise shade of eye-hurting blue customarily worn by the Mentalists of Ning, a race of Mind Worshippers who lived to the west of the Free City of Chx.

"It is potent?" asked Wolf Turgo. When Palensus Choy tested it and signified that it was, he suggested that the old Immortal activate the talisman.

Choy enunciated a Word and Ganelon looked down to discover that he was scraping the gummy residue of stale, rancid fishstew from a chipped ceramic bowl and sipping tepid fayowaddy tea from a cracked mug.

He looked around him with amazement written upon his normally expressionless features. The room was thick with dust and mold, littered with dead leaves, squalid with garbage. The entire throng of brilliant courtiers vanished, leaving a dozen or so unwashed, oafish-looking men, slatternly, sour-faced women, and grubby urchins, munching without enthusiasm on similarly unappetizing fare. The throne at the end of the hall held not the bearded, serenely majestic Emperor but an obese and cretinous bulk attended by seven toothless scarecrows.

"My Claws and Whiskers!" gasped the Tigerman in alarm.

"Oh, dear me," murmurred Palensus Choy.

"What does this mean?" Ganelon demanded of the Ximchak, who watched their dismay and astonishment with a wolfish, leering grin.

"Come to my room after the banquet so we can talk in private, and I'll explain everything," said Wolf Turgo.

As soon as they could possibly do so, Choy, Silvermane, Grrff, Kurdi, and the sphinx-girl excused themselves and retired to their suite. Once the palace seemed to have settled down for the night, they left the luxuriously appointed apartment and found their way to the similar accommodations which had earlier been reserved for the Ximchak delegation.

They had occupied the interlude of time by testing again and again the efficacy of the Ukwukluk scarab in exposing the dingy and repulsive reality behind this amazing illusion. By means of the amulet it was discovered that their suite was a filthy hovel built on the hillside where the rear of the palace lay open to the elements, that their sumptuous couches were rickety cots, and that similar deceptions had cloaked the actuality of all of the furnishings and appointments of their rooms.

Arriving at the Ximchak suite (actually a flimsy lean-to built up against another section of the hillside pockmarked by fetid latrine trenches, and topped with a leaky roof), they discovered Wolf Turgo arguing with the warriors of his retinue, who regarded them sullenly, with suspicion in their surly manner. Apparently, the Ximchaks disliked the notion of fraternizing with the enemy, although as Turgo expressed it, both the Ximchaks and Choy's party were just about in the same boat, as far as the present situation went.

He got directly to the point.

"You already knew that Trancore was a nation of hereditary madmen before you came here, but *we* didn't," he said. "Zaar the Warlord sent me here to feel out the Trancorian mood and their defenses, before further committing the Horde's strength in an attack that might prove as disastrous as our assaults on Valardus and on Mount Naroob. I got stuck with this sticky job sort of as punishment for letting you fellows wipe out my command with that Flying Castle of yours."

"What about the illusory nature of—" began Choy.

"Coming to that now," said Wolf brusquely. "It's very simple: *These people are so completely mad that they believe in their own delusions. Utterly.* Their wacky convictions are so strong that it affects any visitors to the environment which they control. Don't ask me why. Maybe because the whole race has been mad for ages, with the identical delusions, which were by repetition somehow reinforced into the status of quasi-reality. Or maybe the Trancorians have telepathic powers and can influence the sensory impressions of their visitors in some subtle manner. Anyway, there's nothing here but about three dozen ragged and half-starved madmen living in the wreckage of a city half underwater and nine-tenths uninhabited."

"I suppose it should have occurred to me earlier," sighed Palensus Choy fretfully. "Remember, my friends, I told you that the Gray Dynasts and their aerial glass ships were mental illusions, created simply by the fact that the seven sages *believed they could?*"

"Why are you telling us all this?" inquired Silvermane. "After all, we are your enemies, come here in the first place to prevent a Ximchak invasion."

"There won't be any invasion," said Wolf Turgo. "There's

nothing to invade! But my problem is: how do I go back to Farzool to talk the Warlord out of knocking over Trancore? He's not going to believe such a crazy story, and I already got one failure on my record, as it is. That's why I'm being so frank about all this. I need your help, and you need mine."

And thus began an extremely unlikely alliance.

20.

A Council of Peace

By now Ganelon Silvermane and his friends were becoming uncomfortably aware of a growing hunger, all the more bothersome in that it was unreasonable, since they had just eaten.

"That just it," grunted Wolf Turgo. "You *haven't* eaten! Or, rather, you didn't eat anywhere near as much as you thought you did. All of those side dishes, the salad, the dessert, the hors d'oeuvres, were fictitious—the products of the Trancorians' loony delusions. All you had, any of you, was a half-bowl or so of last week's fish stew. Yargash, break out the grub."

"But Wolf—" protested one of the Ximchak officers.

"Yargash, the *grub*."

Grumbling, the warrior opened a cloth sack behind the settee and brought out some roast fowl. It was cold by now, of course, but tender, succulent, delicious. As the members of Ganelon's party gnawed away hungrily, Wolf Turgo explained that once he had discovered that the illusory nature of Trancore extended even to the meals they served here, he had been sending out his warriors every morning to hunt for game. They had, however, a limited supply of real food, only enough to last until tomorrow.

"We got six mouths to feed right here," he grunted. "And with you lot, that's four more empty bellies. Not counting that talking lion of yours; the Stars know how much grub it'll take to fill up anything *that* big!"

"In other words, you've got to be getting back to Gompland," mumbled Grrff around a mouthful of gamebird. "Whereat exactly is this here Warlord of yours holed up, anyway?"

"In Jurago. That's the capital of the Gomps, or it was, anyway. What's left of it, that is. Ol' Zaar, he's sitting pretty in the Barzoolian Palace, killing time by wooing Ruzara—"

"Whozzat?" chirped Kurdi brightly. The boy had lost all his trepedation toward the Ximchaks, finding it impossible to fear people who gave you food to eat.

"The former Queen, cub," grinned Wolf Turgo. "Princess, that is—'fraid we knocked off her royal uncle, Tharzash, when we took over. The Gomps don't actually have kings and queens, y'know, not in the regular sense, that is. They regard millionaires the way most folks regard aristocrats, and the richest among them is the King."

"The system is properly called a plutocracy," murmured Palensus Choy, wiping his lips and fingers on a bit of cloth. "Rule by the wealthy."

"Izzat a fact?" Wolf Turgo continued. "Anyway, once Tharzash got killed, Princess Ruzara was next in line for the throne, or whatever they call it over there. Feisty wench, that Ruzara; a real looker, too. Got a younger sister named Mavella, all snow and ice to Ruzara's spice and fire. Zaar kept them both alive for some reason."

"The King of the Gomps is known as the Regulus Plutarchus, and a Queen would be called the Regina Plutarchas," noted Choy absently. "Do I understand you properly, sir, that you are trying to suggest that we accompany you on your return journey into Gompland?"

Turgo shrugged humorously. "I dunno *what* I'm trying to suggest, old fellow," he admitted. "I'd say yes, and promise you safe conduct, but I'm not sure the Warlord would honor any such commitment made by me. Especially once he finds out you are the same fellows that were responsible for chopping our men into mincemeat before Valardus, and squashed the rest of 'em under that Flying Castle of your atop Mount Naroob! Zaar only respects Horde Law when it suits him to do so; the moment he has a good reason for ignoring this law or that one, they go out the window. The only thing I know is that he's getting desperate, and that he and Barzik can't hold the lid down much longer—"

"Barzik?" inquired Grrff.

"Lord of the Gurko tribe, Zaar's chief supporter," explained the chieftain. From the disparagement in his tones, you might have gathered that he did not exactly consider Barzik his best chum.

"Why 'desperate'?" Ganelon asked, trying to absorb all of this at once.

"We've just about eaten everything there is to eat in Gompland," said Wolf Turgo. "Except for the Gomps, of course. It's quite a huge country, and heavily populated, but you can't move in with a quarter of a million invaders, even to such a big place as Gompland, without cutting into the food supply. And it sure is big.* But the Horde is beginning to get hungry, and when that many warriors start hearing their stomachs growlings, there's going to be an awful lot of trouble unless they get fed."

"In other words, Zaar has to take some decisive course of action, and fast, or he's in trouble, is that it?" asked Ganelon thoughtfully.

"That's about the way things are," the Ximchak admitted. "Thing is, he led us into a sort of cul-de-sac, going into Gomp territory that way. The only way south through that mountain ring that surrounds the place is through the pass that Mount Naroob overlooks, and your Flying Castle blocks that path *very* effectively. Even if Zaar could get past your castle, he'd still be locked in between impassable mountains. The only road to the south is the Luzar Pass that cuts through the High Carthazians. And lo an' behold, you got that one blocked, too, with that murderous moving town of yours, the one that turned us into sausagemeat before Valardus!"†

Ganelon frowned, saying nothing.

"Now, they got plenty of passes leading through the Embosch range into Trancore, but the ones which afford easy passage through the mountains to the east open out on the burning sands of Xoroth, the Fire Desert. The only way to cross that hellish place is on those raised stone causeways the Tensors of Pluron built half a million years ago. Nothing much in that direction; but Trancore looks easy, and rich to boot. So Zaar sent us to look over the lay of the land, before committing the Horde."

"Just what does he think he has to fear here in Trancore?" snorted Grrff the Tigerman derisively.

"He wasn't sure, I guess," admitted Turgo candidly.

---

*The Gompish Regime was about the same size as modern France.

†Obviously, Wolf Turgo (and the leadership of the Horde) had no knowledge of the fact that Kan Zar Kan was no longer blocking the mouth of the Luzar Pass.

"Ages ago, in case you didn't know, the Trancorian Empire was very adequately protected, yes indeed. Ol' Zaar, he wasn't certain but what things were still the same hereabouts."

Palensus Choy cleared his throat in order to intrude upon the conversation.

"Ahem! I believe that I understand what our ruffianly young friend refers to," he murmured vaguely. "Quite some ages ago, before the Safetilian Dilemma exerted its fatal attraction upon the Trancorian intelligentsia, in the days when Trancore was the mightiest and the most magnificent of all metropoli, the Empire was protected by an invisible, man-killing, impenetrable barrier, devised on commission by the Fabricators of Dirdanx, a race of scientific sages of inestimable skill."

"Oh, yeah?" grunted Grrff truculently. "What kind of a barrier?"

"A mile-high zone of unbreathable vacuum, half a mile in width," Choy said. "Nothing that lived, no matter how protected, could penetrate it by more than a dozen yards. That was the barrier which rendered obsolete the former Trancorian practice of maintaining a standing army."

"Ga-*len*-dil!" breathed the Xombolian, hackles bristling.

"Precisely, my dear fellow," said the magician, quietly.

Ganelon had heard of such a thing before, and so had Grrff. For in Karjixia there was a giant vacuum-bubble, called the Death Zone, believed drawn down to the surface of Old Earth by the comet whose head had formed the Air Mines.

The Death Zone of Karjixia, however, was a natural phenomenon. The idea of an artificially manufactured Vacuum Barrier extending around an entire country the size of Trancore, was, to say the very least, unheard of.

"Ain't there no more, huh?" inquired Kurdi interestedly.

"Isn't there," corrected Grrff automatically, and on his very heels, verbally speaking, Ganelon murmured, "Any more."

Palensus Choy shook his head. "Vanished as soon as the Dirdanxian civilization was extinguished by the Pink Plague," he said reminiscently.

"Something's bothering me about all of this," Silvermane spoke up. "Why are we so worried about these Trancorians, anyway? If their imaginations are so powerful as to conjure up the illusion of a city, why couldn't they imagine themselves protected by a large and powerful armed host, strong enough to deter even the Ximchak Horde?"

"I see no reason why they couldn't," Choy said offhandedly. "But it would never occur to them to do so. Lost in their fond dreams of an imperial past, they probably conceive of themselves as still being sheltered by the Vacuum Barrier."

"But they aren't, heh?" mused Grrff. "Howcum? If they got minds strong enough to make us taste food that isn't there, why can't they choke to death an invading army with imaginary vacuum?"

Palensus Choy shook his head.

"Impossible, my dear fellow! Convincing the taste buds of a visitor or two that he is lunching on rare viands is one thing, a mere telepathic influencing of certain neuronic circuitry. But even their delusions are not powerful enough to displace a half a mile of Old Earth's atmosphere!"

"I guess it *is* asking a bit much of the human imagination, to be able to asphyxiate a quarter of a million fighting men purely by mental suggestion," admitted Ganelon gloomily.

"C'n't we tell them t' think up a army?" piped Kurdi.

"Couldn't," said Grrff and Ganelon in unison, under their breaths.

"Impossible, child," sighed Choy. "There is nothing in all this world more difficult than to persuade a madman that he is, in fact, mad. And in order to convince the Trancorians to imagine an illusory army, we would need to convince them the Vacuum Barrier has fallen."

Ganelon got up, stretching, smothering a yawn.

"Let's adjourn this talk till tomorrow," he suggested. "In the meanwhile, we'll sleep on these things and see what's to be done."

But tomorrow proved too busy for further discussion.

For one thing, they woke up to find an army invading them!

21.

A Council of War

It was Ishgadara to whom belonged the credit for discovery of the invading army. The sphinx-girl, easily bored by inaction, found talking about things much less interesting than doing them. So, on the morning after Wolf Turgo had broached the notion of an alliance between him and his retinue and the members of Silvermane's party, she awoke at dawn. Feeling restless, she decided to indulge herself and stretch her wings a bit by taking what she called "a morningk fly."

Peering in at the window, she discovered Ganelon stretched out on his back, snoring thunderously, and Kurdi cuddled beside him in the huge bed, still sound asleep, curled around a fluffy pillow. Ishgadara had hoped to find the little boy already awake, for she had grown fond of the lively, likable child, and knew that he would have enjoyed sharing her morning fly. But he was still asleep, and she did not care to disturb him.

So she strolled out onto the upper slopes of the Bryza above the palace complex. The great golden Sun had barely risen above the horizon, and the first few shafts of dawnlight were blazing through the Embosch Mountains, which blocked the eastern landscape like a wall built by giants. The Sun was cooler and dimmer by this age than it had been in our own, its white fires darkened into gold; but then, it was seven hundred million years older, and some lessening of its vigor was only to be expected.

The air was crisp and cool, the grass damp with dew, and all of the heavens to the west were still drowned in darkness, and bore up the last few sleepy stars which do not flee the skies until the Sun is well up.

Stretching like a giant cat, the sphinx-girl opened her bronze-feathered wings like an enormous fan, then sprang into the air and soared aloft in a lazy spiral. The countryside to the east of the sea were thick with purple shadows, but the first light of morning already glittered in the slow, heavy waters of the Wryneck, where it came meandering down from the mountains which marked the western borders of Gompland and crossed the plains to mingle with the Greater Pommernarian Sea.

Just beyond the mountainous rampart, Ishgadara's keen eyes caught the twinkle of polished steel. Intrigued, she inclined her flight toward the east.

Then she saw them. A vast host of mounted warriors were negotiating the Marjid Pass, which penetrated the Embosch range at the very foot of Thunder Troll Mountain. A huge number of the warriors, either mounted astride orniths or riding in war chariots drawn by clumsy, lumbering scarlet lizards called *nguamadon*, had already reached this side of the mountains, and were assembling into battle formation.

Ishgadara had seen the Ximchaks from a distance at the Siege of Valardus, and she had fought them face to face during the attack on Mount Naroob. So there was no mistaking them in their black leather armor and fur cloaks, their helmets crowned with Youk antlers, their weird scarlet eyes ringed with green paint. Nor was there any possibility of mistaking their intention in marching through the Marjid Pass into the Trancorian Empire.

Quite obviously, the dissatisfaction and grumbling among the Ximchaks, which Wolf Turgo had described to Ganelon and his companions during their council the night before, had grown during the days he had been absent from Jurago. To control the rising tide of discontent, the Warlord Zaar must have chosen not to wait for a final report from his embassy, but to lead the Horde, or a sizable portion of it, over into Trancorian territory.

"Petter pe tellingk this to master," the sphinx-girl muttered to herself. Soaring low over the host, in order to ascertain the number and disposition of the invaders, she then turned about and slanted her strong bronze-colored wings back in the direction of the palace of Scaviolis again.

To be invaded at all is not good news, but to be invaded before breakfast is downright uncivilized! Such, at least, was the opinion voiced by Palensus Choy. He stood on the battlements of the topmost tier of the palace, peering down the other side of Bryza hill and across the suburbs of Trancore, which were submerged beneath the waters of the sea.

He still wore his nightshirt, and, although he had wrapped his skinny form in a heavy blanket fetched from his bedroll, the dank morning breeze was uncomfortably chill as it blew up his hem and upon his bare legs. He shivered, and sneezed.

Ishgadara had returned, rousing them with her hoarse bellowings of alarm. Standing now on the parapets of the palace, with Grrff the Xombolian and Ganelon Silvermane and little Kurdi, the old magician sniffed miserably, wondering if he was catching cold.

The army had passed through the Marjid by now, and the rough estimate of its number surpassed ten thousand. Which was more than the Warlord had dispatched against Valardus and Zaradon added together. Zaar, obviously, had learned by now not to underestimate his enemies.

And this time they did not even have the Flying Castle to contend with.

The Ximchak host had gathered into a fighting formation shaped like a giant chevron or broad-based arrowhead. They were presently riding across the Ovarva Plains, and the outriders of the host had already reached the shores of the Wryneck River. They were still too far away to be visible to the unaided eye, of course, but Palensus Choy was magician enough to command the Air Elementals to magnify the scope of vision so that, while the spell lasted, they could clearly observe the forces of the enemy.

Wolf Turgo lounged against the parapet, looking unhappy. Because of the magnification of their vision, he was able to make out the gux-tail standard amid the host, which signified that it was led by Qarziger the Red, one of the chiefs of the Horde with whom he did not enjoy the friendliest of relations. This same Qarziger was reckoned among the more hostile and belligerent of the Ximchak leaders, and had a peculiar fondness for beheading his foes and fashioning their skulls into winecups from which he delighted to drink to their memories. He had, by now, Wolf Turgo remembered gloomily, quite a collection of these gruesome goblets.

"It'll take 'em a while to find a way across that river," growled Grrff to Ganelon. "Doesn't seem very deep, but it sure is broad. They'll hafta ride all the way back to that gooseneck curve, back over there, to bring across the chariots and wagons."

Ganelon nodded somberly. "Still and all, they'll be across by early afternoon, and encamped along the seashore before evening. I wish we had the Flying Castle with us."

"Sure would help," admitted Grrff. "But there's no use cryin' over castles what ain't here! Lissen, big man, maybe the sea itself'll stop 'em. No bridges or causeways across it, on account of it's too big.* So how they gonna get to the island, anyway?"

Ganelon extended one arm and pointed to a forest of considerable extent, called the Urrach by the Trancorians, which stood in the northerly parts of the plain.

"They'll cut down trees and use the logs to float across, most likely," he grunted. "Still, it will take time, and they will only be able to bring a small portion of their force against the island itself."

"Wish we had some o' them *bombs*," muttered little Kurdi, referring to the explosives Ollub Vetch had employed with such efficacy against the Naroob invaders.

"Yes, they'd come in handy, that's for sure," said Grrff.

"*Those* bombs," said Ganelon.

By sundown the army was encamped in a great half-circle about the shores of the Greater Pommernarian Sea. The Trancorians, who lived mainly on fish, although their systematic delusions convinced them otherwise, had a few dilapidated fishing boats, but these were drawn up to the edges of the island of Trancore itself. There was no way for the Ximchaks to cross the inland sea.

So there, for a time, at least, the situation stood in stalemate.

That night Ganelon Silvermane and Palensus Choy strove with all the ingenuity they possessed to impress upon their hosts the dangerousness of the peril afforded by the Ximchak presence. They got nowhere. The madness of the Trancorians was a highly selective one: they saw what they expected to see, and, conversely, did not see what they did not expect to see. This included the Ximchak host encamped across the water: to them it simply was not there, because it *could*

---

*The Greater Pommernarian Sea was roughly one hundred miles across at its broadest extent.

not be. The Vacuum Barrier still stood, in their determined imaginations.

Over the next four days the Ximchaks busied themselves by cutting down trees from the edges of the Urrach and tying the logs together into crude but serviceable rafts. By now they must have realized that all was not exactly kosher in Trancore—three-quarters of the city was underwater, and while the remainder of the metropolis presented a detailed, realistic, and sustained illusion of luxuriousness at its height, prolonged observation must have revealed to the keen-eyed Barbarians that the streets were empty of palanquins, chariots, crowds, or just plain passersby, and that no smoke rose from the chimneys, no guards paced the parapets, and that Trancore was—must be—ninety-nine percent deserted. Still they pressed on with the construction of the miniature navy of rafts.

It was only a matter of time.

Since they could not arouse in the Trancorians any sense of danger, Ganelon turned to Wolf Turgo. A council of war was held during which a variety of means and measures were discussed. Wolf knew he was in trouble, if not from one direction, then from another. He should have reported back to Jurago or Farzool by messenger pigeon that the city was all but uninhabited. That he had not done so would probably be interpreted by the Warlord Zaar as an indication that he had gone over to the side of the enemy.

By the morning of the fifth day, rafts full of Ximchaks had set out from the shoreline, and the battle of Trancore began.

Book Four

AGAINST THE XIMCHAKS

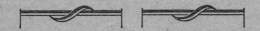

The Scene: Island Trancore in the Greater
Pommernarian Sea; the Wryneck River;
the Urrach; the Ovarva Plains.

New Characters: Qarziger the Red, Black
Unggo, Harsha of the Horn; the shaman
Kishtu, and other Ximchaks; Princess
Ruzara of Jurago.

22.

The Battle of the Bryza

The first attack came that morning. Red Qarziger had cunningly launched his raft navy during the night while darkness still lay thickly upon the sea. By dawn the rafts had reached the outermost of the buildings of Trancore, which were on the edges of the city. Here only the roofs of the houses, or at most an upper story, stood up out of the water. Here the streets went meandering down into the waves. Qarziger found it easy to pole the rafts up one of these empty streets, drag the rafts up out of the shallows, then advance up the street toward Trancore's capitol hill afoot.

Ganelon had expected something of the sort, and had posted guardwatch on the parapets of the Bryza palace. Unfortunately for the defenders of Trancore, the Ximchaks had timed the whole thing to a nicety, and the tribal shamans among the host, who had some smattering of starry lore, it seemed, selected a night for the attack when the skies were moonless.*

So accustomed were the inhabitants of Gondwane in this age to the brilliant luminosity of the immense Moon, by which you could easily have read the fine print of newspaper columns, if they had still had newspapers in Ganelon's age, which they didn't, that the occasional night when the laggard Moon lingered below the horizon instead of floating up over the edges of the world to flood the landscape with its dazzling glare seemed to the Gondwanians one of impenetrable gloom.

---

*During the long ages the Falling Moon had drawn much closer to Old Earth than in our time, with the result that the stronger gravitational pull dragged against the satellite, slowing its flight. Hence every month there were moonless nights.

Thus, even though Grrff was on guard at the time, and with his cat's eyes should have been able to see through the murk sufficiently to spy the invaders and sound the alarm, he couldn't and didn't. The first thing he knew about the Ximchak landing was when a lasso settled about his upper torso and jerked him off his feet. Then black figures clambered up over the parapets, their antler-crowned helmets blotting out the few, faint stars.

The Ximchaks had never faced a Tigerman before, or they would have realized that you can't lasso somebody with claws four inches long and keen as razors. *Snikk* went those terrible talons, slicing through the tough rope, and the Xombolian was free. Voicing a guttural roar that froze the Barbarians in their tracks, the Tigerman was upon them in one lithe, blurred pounce. Tiger-eyes ablaze, Grrff struck out with balled, furry fists like mauls. Ximchaks fell like ninepins; then he pounced upon his ygdraxel, did Grrff, and that terrible weapon flashed and glittered in the torchlight as it struck and struck and struck again. With his free hand Grrff, whose presence of mind was also catlike, reached out and struck the alarm gong.

In another moment of two they had him circled in, and a dozen scimitars flashed for his striped breast. But a naked giant like a bronze colossus loomed up behind them to seize the bowlegged little men by the scruff of their necks and toss them over the parapet. It was Ganelon Silvermane, who slept without a nightshirt, and hadn't bothered to dress after being awakened by the alarm gong sounded.

Before this grim apparition that melted out of thin air and tossed full-grown men around as if they were dolls, the Ximchaks chose discretion over valor and bolted for their scaling ladders. Some didn't bother with the ladders, but jumped, trusting to a soft landing on their comrades bunched below.

Ganelon and Grrff helped the others down by throwing the ladders off-balance. Then the parapet was free of Ximchaks and the two had a breathing space, but only for a moment.

For noise farther on around the parapet demonstrated to them that Qarziger the Red was not completely ignorant of rudimentary siege tactics. He had, in fact, sent men to scale the parapets of the Bryza palace at all seven of its sides, and at the same time.

The noises, though, were shouts of alarm, fear, and oaths of dismay. For the gong had also aroused Palensus Choy from his slumbers, and, as the advance wave of Ximchaks were just then learning, it is never very smart to waken magicians abruptly from their sleep: they can be very, *very* irritable.

In this particular incident, Choy's irritability took the shape of ball lightning. Glimmering globes of unearthly electric fire swelled into being between the horns of his ivory caduceus, which he sent rolling along the parapet, skipping and bouncing erratically. When one of these rolling globes of scintillant force came into contact with Ximchak toes, knees, shinbones or whatever, the results were identical with what you might feel if you struck your finger into a light socket and turned the switch to *on*.

At the risk of a bad pun, the Epic says of this episode that the Ximchaks found the experience extremely shocking.

Grrff and Ganelon had both jumped to the same conclusion—that the parapet was being hit from all sides simultaneously—and they ran off down the parapet in opposite directions, and each ran straight into a band of marauders. This was all right in Grrff's case, since he carried his ygdraxel: he just waded in and started ripping. Ganelon's case was a trifle different, though, since he had gotten out of the bedroom in such a hurry that he had forgotten to snatch up the Silver Sword. So he had to grab the nearest Ximchak and use him in lieu of a club, as a sort of blunt instrument, swinging him around by his heels. Swung Ximchak proved a very effective cudgel or bludgeon; however, the cudgel itself did not survive the wear and tear of prolonged usage, and soon Ganelon had to select another blunt instrument from among his adversaries.

Cracklings and sizzle-*pop!*s from around the curve of the parapet suggested that Palensus Choy had similarly encountered another Ximchak gang to amuse himself with.

The problem of a worthy weapon was solved by about the time that Ganelon had used his second bludgeon until it was no longer in the finest condition. Little Kurdi came panting to the parapet, lugging the Silver Sword. The boy had been snoozing in the buff like Ganelon, and his bare brown body gleamed in the orange flare of the torches. Ganelon did not approve of this and tried to get him to wear the Gondwanish equivalent of pajamas, but it was difficult for him to enforce this as he usually dozed off before Kurdi did.

Snatching up the Silver Sword with a happy word of thanks, Ganelon crashed into the mob of Ximchaks and slaughtered them to the last man. Then, telling Kurdi to get

back downstairs out of harm's way, he went further down the
parapet. By now the upper tier of the palace was crawling
with Ximchaks, thick as vermin.

By dawn the battle was in full swing. Ishgadara, who
was hard to awaken under the best of circumstances, woke
at last and threw her not inconsiderable weight behind the
defense of the Bryza. She flew around the outside walls,
knocking flat every scaling ladder she could see. This prevented any further incursion of the savage warriors; there
remained only the job of eliminating those who had already
gotten in.

It was Palensus Choy who saved the day. Sorcerers use
their Third Eye, situated in the forebrain, to see the auric
radiation of men on the plane of astral vision. The Third Eye
works through walls or any other barrier, so one by one as
Choy located a Ximchak, and Grrff or Ganelon rooted him
out and rendered him *hors de combat*.

It took most of the morning.

The rest of the Ximchaks, unable to scale the walls with
Ishgadara maintaining her terrible vigilance, contented themselves with looting and gutting and burning the lesser buildings of the city. This was small loss, actually, since the buildings were mere empty shells, palatial hovels filled with garbage.

Once the Bryza was Ximchak-free, the defenders mounted
Ishgadara and harried the rest of the invasion force back to
their rafts from above. Ball lightning, although it rarely killed,
proved every bit as effective as Ollub Vetch and his bombs
in routing Ximchaks and panicking them into a stampede.

The Ximchaks took to the sea in their rafts, trying to
bring down the sphinx-girl with their arrows. This got
Ishgadara hopping mad, and a ton and a half of angry fifteen-
foot-long sphinx is a lot of mad. She relieved her temper for
a while by ripping the rooftiles from half-submerged villas
and dropping these on the crowded rafts from a considerable
height. If you do this in just the right way, she soon discovered, you can knock rafts apart into floating logs. In time she
got really expert in this little-known art, breaking up some
thirty-two rafts by Grrff's own count.

She discovered something else, too.

Ximchaks didn't know how to swim.

As for Red Qarziger, he had insisted on going along with
the invasion force, instead of staying behind in his tent like
most generals. He never came back. A large enough roofing

tile, dropped from a sufficient height, cracks open even a general's helmet, to say nothing of his skull.

When Ishgadara ran out of roofs, Palensus Choy took over with the ball lightning again, which worked just as well at breaking rafts apart. By noontime, or just before, the Ximchaks had lost over five hundred warriors, to say nothing of forty-three rafts. Now they would have to start all over.

The defenders of Trancore, having destroyed the last raft, flew back to the Bryza palace for a late, and very large, breakfast. They had well earned it.

23.

Time Out for the Flower Boats

It was really, reflected Kurdi to himself, pretty darn *weird!* Here Ganelon Silvermane and Grrff the Xombolian and the Immortal of Zaradon—and even Ishgadara the sphinx-girl —were closeted half the afternoon, worrying over how to save Trancore from being grabbed by the savage Ximchaks, discussing and arguing over courses of possible action, and all the while the Trancorians themselves were going about their normal business as if nothing out of the way unusual was happening at all. *Weird!*

As a matter of fact, this very afternoon the lords and viziers and grandees of the Imperial Court, most of whom were purely illusory in every sense of the word, were attending the gala fete and festival which was the annual Trancorian Flower Boat Regatta. Sitting alone on the parapet, hugging one bare brown knee and letting the other leg dangle carelessly down over the wall, the boy watched raptly as ornate, floridly bedecked gondolas circled the island city, languidly cheered on by the nobles, who waved colored scarves and silken handkerchiefs in a restrained manner, by way of egging on the contestants of their choice.

On the distant shore, the Ximchaks strained their eyes, trying to figure out what was going on and what all the commotion was about. When the flower-wreathed gondolas had first appeared to their view, the suspicious Ximchaks had, as was only reasonable, feared a counterattack by sea. Now they gawped incredulously as languid youths and listless maidens poled pleasure-boats bedight with many-colored blossoms in lazy circles around and around the island. It made Kurdi giggle to himself.

In one hand he held the Ukwukluk scarab, which the old

magician had let him borrow and had shown him how to use. From time to time the lad employed the powers latent within the amulet to dispel the illusions projected or induced by the Mad Trancorians. When he did so, the graceful boats and gay throngs vanished into thin air as if by magic. All that remained of the gorgeous, festive throng was a couple of dozen tatterdemalion scarecrows staring rheumily out to the empty waves and flapping their bony arms like the loonies they were.

Weird! thought Kurdi, hugging his knees.

Across the water, the Ximchaks stared upon the spectacle with surly suspicion, truculent contempt, and belligerent bewilderment. They couldn't figure out whether the Trancorians were showing off or bluffing.

"The pompous dogs do be a-tauntin' us with they invincibility," growled Black Unggo sourly. "They know we can't get to um, and do be playin' to git us mad." Unggo, a beefy individual with a thick curly blue-black beard, had inherited the feather-plumed crest of the war-chief, which now adorned his antlered helm, upon the instant the rooftile had dashed out the brains of Red Qarziger.

An eager-eyed flunky with rotting teeth who stood next to him nodded obsequiously. "They be mockin' of us, you right, chief!" he burbled. "You sure hit um on the nose *thet* time! Boy, if'n us could on'y git over thar, we'd sure make um mock outa th' other side o' they faces."

This particular specimen of Ximchak manhood, one Iquanux by name, had been agreeing with every word spoken by Unggo the Black since he inherited the leadership of the expedition. To make certain no one failed to understand how vigorously he supported whatever side Black Unggo took on any given question, and how intensely he admired his chief's shrewdness and perspicacity, he generally underscored his words by giving several vehement nods, which he did now.

Iquanux, you understand, had been Qarziger's second-in-command, and felt his position of authority to be hanging by a thread.

"Maybe it's not that at all, chief," suggested a keen-eyed bright-looking young Ximchak in a mild voice. His name was Harsha, and he was called Harsha of the Horn because of the huge coiled brass trumpet he wore tossed over one shoulder, it being his duty to sound the advance.

"Huh?" demanded Unggo gloomily. "What else hit *be*, then?"

"Yeah, what else *c'd* hit be; th' chief be right!" Iquanux chimed in, glaring around in a challenging manner, if as daring anybody else to disagree with Unggo.

"Oh, I don't know," shrugged Harsha negligently. "Might be a religious thingy, I suppose. Giving thanks to their Gods for the victory, you know, that sort of thing—"

"The Trancorian swine *have* no Gods, the atheistical pigs," spoke up a thin-lipped oldster bitterly. This was Kishtu, the tribal shaman of the Gurko clan, to whom had been given the honor—and also the obligation—of destroying Trancore.

"No gods at all, eh?" asked Harsha of the Horn.

"None, curse the heresy!" snapped Kishtu. "They posses from of old one of the most antique and authentic likenesses of Galendil the Good, but abandoned his worship many ages ago. The idol is fifteen *farangs* in height, fashioned out of solid silver, and virgin silver, at that!"

"Silver, eh?" mumbled Black Unggo. Cupidity gleamed in his little piggish eyes at the thought of the precious metal and the wealth it represented. He licked his lips.

Sensing the drift of his chief's thought, Iquanux turned on one of the runners. "How do Larx's boys be a-doin' wif cuttin' them new rafts, you?" he inquired loudly. "Chief Unggo, him ain' gonna wait till th' Moon falls, t' git over thar!"

"Have um ready two, three days," replied the runner.

"Silver, eh?" repeated Unggo hungrily. You could tell he was slow to finish thinking about Topic A, and slower still to go on to thinking about Topic B. Particularly so when Topic A was about treasure. "Why silver, I wunner. Not gol'?"

"All statues of God Galendil are made from silver," grated the shaman Kishtu harshly. "It is the metal sacred to Galendil; when the God appeared to the Prophet Phoy in person during what is called the Phoyish Apparition, eyewitnesses reported that the Divinity resembled a majestic, bearded man entirely colored silver."

"Silver's *nice*," grunted Unggo lasciviously.

"So's *gol'*, eh chief?" suggested toady Iquanux, with a conspiratorial leer.

"Gol's nice, *too*," agreed Unggo. The two sniggered nastily, exchanging leers. And Iquanux relaxed a little, feeling his job was a bit more secure than it had been.

Harsha of the Horn wandered off through the throng of staring, muttering, neck-craning Ximchaks. He was a different sort from the older chiefs, of the same younger, more intelligent and alert and personable generation as Wolf Turgo, one of his friends. The chiefs and men of the former generation were true Barbarians—unwashed, slovenly, pigheaded, thick-witted, and oafish. All they liked were the gross physical pleasures of bashing in heads, swilling tubs of beer, and tupping as many wenches as they could corner. Harsha's sort were almost civilized. If he ever thought about the difference between the Ximchak generations, which he seldom did, Harsha might have recognized the obvious: Unggo's generation had been half-grown boys when Zaar's father had roused them from the wearisome stupor of nomadic hunting and whipped them into a war force capable of conquering the world.

They could not be expected to have changed over the years. But Harsha and Wolf Turgo and the other younger men had not even been born back in the days when the nascent Horde wandered the grasslands between the Twin Rivers, Xim and Chak. They had been raised on the warmarch; their education had been achieved in the rubble of the seventy civilizations the Horde had squashed.

And you cannot be exposed to civilization, even slightly, without becoming slightly civilized yourself.

Harsha observed a beautiful young girl and ambled over to join her. Her raven hair was sleek as silk, long as a banner. Her complexion was clear, tanned, healthy. Her eyes were bright golden jewels, strange, brilliant, haunting. Her trim, boyish figure and long coltish legs and firm, pointed breasts had long intrigued him. She wore tight trousers of forest-green, suede boots, a close-fitted leather jerkin. Over one shoulder was slung an unstrung bow and quiver of arrows. She was the Gompish Princess, Ruzara, brought along as a hostage. The two Gompish Princesses were the "guests" of the dominant Gurko clan; the younger, Mavella, was held in the palace at Jurago, and the older had been made to accompany the clan in the field. A born Amazon, out of place among her peaceable people, Ruzara had adjusted to clan life and to war with something like enthusiasm.

"Did you see the boats?" inquired Harsha as he approached the girl.

"Damn the boats!" said Ruzara, looking bloodthirsty. "How are *our* boats coming? I mean, *your* boats—"

"No," grinned the young man. "You mean 'our' boats. Princess, you should have been a Ximchak! I swear it: sometimes I think you're better suited to clan life than—well, than I am."

"I can believe it," she sniffed, tossing her head in a way he found bewitching. She cast a contemptuous look at his coiled horn. "All you do is sound the assault," she grimaced. "*I* will join the fray, and Gompish arrows will for once slay on the Ximchak side!"

They exchanged a few more words before he ambled off to find his tent. Ruzara was bewitching, but a tiger-cat, all bristles and claws, no cuddle or coo. And there were times when Harsha felt like cuddle and coo.

Ruzara was not for him, obviously.

The next day, however, war was resumed. And Harsha used his horn and Ruzara her arrows.

24.

Battle on the Ovarva Plains

The council of war was soon over. There wasn't much to decide, because there wasn't very much that they could do to defend Trancore. Two warriors, one little boy, an old magician, and a talking lion-lady with wings simply cannot fight off an army.

Or *could* they?

"We sure could use that dang Wolf Turgo you like so much," grumbled Grrff. "Wish he'd come over to our side; but ol' Grrff's afraid he's on 'tother."

"At least he didn't interfere when they attacked the palace last night," Ganelon said pointedly. "He could have knifed us in the back, if he'd wanted to."

"Okay, I'll give him that," said the Tigerman grudgingly. "On the other hand, he didn't exactly help us, either."

As a matter of simple fact, Wolf Turgo had stayed out of the whole affair, staunchly maintaining that he had been asleep the whole time.

"And yer men too, Grrff supposes?" inquired that worthy sarcastically.

"Them too," smiled the Ximchak easily.

"Hrrmph!" was Grrff's only rejoinder.

Rather than just to sit tight, waiting for the Ximchaks to build more rafts and make a second attempt to seize the Bryza, Ganelon's companions had voted to bring the war to the enemy where he least suspected it.

So, the evening of the Flower Boat Regatta, Ishgadara flew out over the Ovarva Plains, with Grrff and Palensus Choy. Their objective was the rope bridge which Qarziger had commanded his men to rig across the easiest ford in the Wryneck River. True, it wasn't much of a bridge, only a taut cable bridging the floods, but it made ford-crossing easier, and the one thing the Ximchaks were most worried about was keeping open their supply line across the Embosch Mountains into Gompish territory.

Two of Choy's ball lightnings, placed just right, eliminated the rope bridge. It was hardly a decisive stroke, but it did make things just that much harder for the Barbarians.

"Pity you can't make the river rise, or bring down an avalanche to block the Marjid," grexed* the Tigerman, referring to the mountain pass the Ximchaks had used to cross over into the Trancorian Empire.

"We can't have everything," sniffed the old magician primly. "And to do either of those things would require the services of a River Elemental or a Snow Elemental. Unfortunately, I have vows of obedience from neither class."

The rope bridge destroyed, they flew north until they were over the Urrach. Here Choy's balls of lightning wreaked havoc among the trees, and started a fire in the forest. The season was the last gasp of fall and the first breath of winter, and the spaces between the trees were choked with fallen leaves, which were as dry as tinder. The fire raged merrily, and pretty soon the wind drove burning sparks and cinders into those parts of the forest where the Ximchaks were busily at work on the new rafts. Before long they came boiling out of the brush, coughing and gagging and slapping sparks from their furs, for all the world like a posse of hornets whose nest has been knocked down.

Circling lazily against the twilight, the defenders of Trancore watched with an immense satisfaction the fury of the Ximchaks, as fire raged on through the Urrach.

By then things were getting a bit too dark to continue, so they flew back home to Trancore and to supper.

"Tomorrow morning, bright an' early, m'lass," grinned Grrff with an affectionate slap at Ishgadara's haunches, "it's up an' at 'em again!"

"Me ready for um," she grinned back.

The next day the defenders of Trancore sowed some more chaos in the Ximchak ranks, again employing Choy's trick lightning balls. They discovered, among other things, that felt

---

*To grex. A term unique to the philology of the Gondwanian language, without a precise equivalent in English. To grouch, gripe, grumble, or grouse, especially in a low, indistinct mutter.

tents burn quite as brightly as forest brush, and that one lightning ball in the right place can stampede a hundred orniths out of their corral. All morning the Barbarians were kept busy waddling breathlessly about the plain, trying to catch their steeds.

By the time they had the stray horse-birds rounded up, they had neither breath left nor time enough to get back to work on the rafts.

They kept this sort of aerial harassment up for two days more. Then, in a manner of speaking, on the third day the roof fell in.

The defenders of Trancore had flown out late that morning astride Ishgadara, loaded for bear. Using his scrying-glass— a small, easily portable crystal Palensus Choy had packed along in his saddlebags before leaving the Flying Castle— the absent-minded magician had discovered that the Ximchaks were felling trees by night and were busily at work constructing the new rafts at hidden places deep within the Urrach forest.

The forest fires begun by Choy's lightning balls some days before had only gnawed at the edges of that immense tract of trees, and had not reduced the entire woods to ash. Armed with this intelligence, and having pinpointed the location of the raft-building sites by astral vision, the old Immortal believed that he could lead Ishgadara to the precise spots where a bit of tame lightning would do the most good. Grrff and Ganelon went along for the ride. So did Kurdi, who adamantly refused to be left out when fun and excitement were in the offing.

There is an old saying which warns about putting all of one's hen fruit in the same wicker container, on the theory that one untimely jostle and you could spill all your yolks at once. Older (quite literally) than the hills, this homely apothegm went disregarded on this particular occasion. And therefrom eventuated considerable heartache and discomfort for all concerned. For the Ximchaks were getting pretty darned tired of being harassed and harried from the air by this time, and yearned to bring their flying foemen down to earth, where they could deal with them on a more man-to-man basis. Toward this much-desired end they employed the peculiar arts of the shaman Kishtu. The witch doctors who accompanied the Horde knew little science and less magic, but they were exceptionally well schooled in the uses of drugs

and poisons. And the shaman Kishtu, he of the thin lips and
bitter manner, possessed a choice formula whose efficacy he
had long desired to test under field conditions.

It was a narcotic which worked like a fast-acting, very
powerful sedative. It was supposed to be able to put a man
to sleep on his feet in an eyeblink. And it had occurred to
Kishtu's cunning and guileful mind that in order to bring
about the much-desired cessation of these winged guerrilla
raids, it was needful only to eliminate the flying lady lion-
creature. The others, he reasoned, could not fly.

An arrow whose head was steeped in the sleepy potion was
obviously the weapon of choice. Consequently, the finest and
most accurate archer in the Ximchak host was selected to
do the honors. This turned out to be the turncoat Gompish
daredevil and girl-spitfire, Princess Ruzara. Her gold eyes
blazed at this opportunity to take a more active part on the
battlefield.

Rather late on the morning of the fourth day after the
Trancorians had held their make-believe Flower Boat Regatta, therefore, when sentries spied the approaching Gynosphinx, the lissom girl archer clambered to the top of a
wucca-wucca tree which towered above the Urrach and
crouched on a leaf-hidden limb, bow strung and ready, and
herself breathless with anticipation.

Ishgadara circled the forest area identified by Choy as the
site of the secret tree-felling and raft-making operation, never
noticing the archeress hidden in the upper boughs of the tall
wucca-wucca tree. The first clue they had that something
was amiss was when the sphinx-girl suddenly wobbled in her
flight and started to descend in a woozy, lopsided spiral.

"Hey!" yelped Grrff, grabbing a pawful of mane. "What's
up? I mean—*down*."

"Sleepy-time," yawned Ishgadara in an indistinct mum-
ble. "Me take-um nappy-nap now. . . ."

Before they could voice further query or protest, she came
down to earth and landed with a bump that spilled them
head over heels onto the turf. Then she rolled over on her
side and began to snore like a sawmill. It was Kurdi who
spotted the bright-green arrow sticking out of her dexter
wing; the shaft had not seriously maimed or injured that member, but it had scratched her flesh. And she was sound
asleep.

Then a howling mob of vengeful Ximchaks burst out of
the underbrush and came at them in a rush from all direc-

tions. There was no time to think or plot of plan, no time to discuss or question or argue or even confer. It was simply a matter of out, sword, and fall to. Which Ganelon and Grrff did in less time than it takes to tell of it.

Clambering down from the tree, Ruzara paused to look, and it was suddenly brought home to her just what she had done. These people were fighting to keep from happening to Trancore the sort of thing which had already happened to her own realm of Gompia. She bit her lip; but there was point in crying over spilled milk or snoozing Gynosphinxes.

25.

Ollub Vetch Intervenes

The Silver Sword was five feet of shimmering, razory metal from cross-hilt to point. And the length, and strength, or the arm which swung it was more than human.

Silvermane planted both booted feet firmly, braced himself, and swung the gigantic broadsword with all the massive force his bronze thews possessed. The blade hissed, slicing the air in a broad arc. At various points along that arc, the first few Ximchaks were in the way. The more impetutous of their fellows, perhaps, or merely the fastest of foot. Well, their running days were over.

The first Ximchaks was sliced neatly in half, just above the pelvis. The second ducked, but not far enough, and his head parted company with the rest of him. The third, a beefy individual with a beer belly, had the misfortune to have the Silver Sword wedge into his spine, it having cut through the rest of him without trouble. Jerking the broadsword free with a practiced twist, Ganelon swung it over his head and brought it down sharply, splitting the fourth man open like a ripe melon.

These four were the first rank. The second rank put on the brakes with all possible urgency, but not swiftly enough to avoid the second lateral sweep of that scythelike supersword.

In no time, like a practiced campaigner, Ganelon had found himself a shelter to fight behind. In his case the barrier was composed of the leaking cadavers of the first seven or eight Ximchaks imprudent enough to venture within reach of his sword.

Grrff, in the meanwhile, had wasted no time at all in whipping out his ygdraxel. A vicious weapon, the Karjixian ygdraxel, and able to deal out nasty wounds when wielded by someone who knows what he is doing. Those inward-pointing hooks, which can be made to *snick* in and out, can do you an injury if you are not careful around ygdraxels being used by angry Tigermen.

The first caterwauling Ximchak to come within Grrff's reach got it in the pit of the stomach, and promptly lost not only his breakfast bit his ability to ever again digest a meal. The second got it in the face, which speedily became a red ruin, which was no great loss to the world of beauty, however it may have distressed the man who had worn it. The third was lucky: he only lost an arm. The fourth and fifth to challenge the hooked horror of the ygdraxel were similarly lucky in the appendage department, or unlucky, it all depending on your point of view.

Grrff was building himself a barrier like Ganelon's.

Palensus Choy had not been idle while these sanguinary events were transpiring about him. The vague, verbose, absent-minded old Immortal (as the two warriors had found out ere this) was swift enough to act when the chips were down. His ivory caduceus had been all primed and ready to start burning up rafts. It was no particular trick to burn up Ximchaks instead.

Palensus Choy had long ago discovered that you can take a lot of the fight out of even a rip-roaring savage with a well-placed jolt of magic-made lightning. The quarters in which they fought were somewhat too closely cramped for ball lightning to be very effective, for the eerily glowing and rather deadly stuff tends to wobble about and meander. But *bolt* lightning is something else again, and goes straight to its mark like a flung spear.

Except that it kills a lot more spectacularly, that is.

The first Ximchak dumb enough to pick the skinny old man for an adversary turned into a human torch on the instant and staggered from the scene, screeching and streaming flames. He had been struck in midleap. The fellow behind him, however, was standing in dew-wet grass when he got his: struck dead as though poleaxed, he toppled, blazing, like a falling tree. The next three to jump on Palensus Choy had also to go through wet grass, and none lived long enough to get a whiff of the singularly unpleasant odor which is your own flesh burning like tinder.

Eighteen men were dead in the first eleven seconds, and the rest promptly lost their enthusiasm for the charge. But behind them were many more, and behind these were their officers—quite a ways behind, of course, being officers. So, however unenthusiastic they may have felt about walking within reach of that shining sword, the ygdraxel, or the lightning-tosser, they waded grimly forward anyway, and died. And died. And died.

All of this Ruzara watched from where she stood frozen by the tree, sweetly lovely face pale, eyes enshadowed with an emotion she could not name.

The Gompish Princess had, originally, no love for the fur-clad invaders who had gutted and looted her realm, leaving the Thirty Cities blackened shells. But she had been born a fighter, a tomboy, a scrapper, and had argued vehemently from the first that her royal father ought to have raised levies and marched to fight the Ximchaks. If Gompland had maintained a standing army, or a trained militia . . . if the seven mountain passes had been blocked by fortresses, with manned garrisons . . . if a lot of things . . . but none of these had been done, and the Gompish Regime fell with a resounding thump.

Contemptuous of her spineless nation, despising its smug—and dead wrong—sense of security, it was only human of the girl, once conquered, to admire in her conquerors those martial virtues lacking in her own people. From admiration to something like hero-worship and the urge that moves the uncommitted toward conversion is a small step, indeed.

Forced to accompany the Gurko clan when they marched against Trancore, for which she cared little or nothing, the girl found herself enjoying it all. There was that in her which liked to swagger and swashbuckle, and the outward trappings of armies are, or can be, intoxicating. There is the feeling of one's individuality being lost, submerged in something greater than oneself: the sense of being part of a vast, overwhelming force.

But it's one thing to gloat vicariously over descriptions of battles in books, and something very different to be in one. Men in pain screamed like gelded horses; guts spill in greasy-white, obscene tangles from slit bellies; men in their death agonies befoul or wet themselves ludicrously and shamefully. Death and murder and the smell of blood and the brassy taste of fear are real and ugly, and it takes a kind of madness to enjoy them.

Ruzara did not enjoy them; not in the slightest.

Her eyes drank in the magnificent manhood of Ganelon

Silvermane as he held twenty men at bay. His grim, scowling face was as devoid of emotion as a mask cut in cold bronze. He revealed no fear, he displayed no pleasure in what he was doing. He fought because he must. Nor did Ruzara miss the fact that many times he took frightful risks, exposing himself to lashing spears and flying blades, so as to shield with his naked body the very small boy huddled behind him.

That which was womanly within her thrilled to the manliness within him, to his male beauty, his daring, his fearlessness, his prowess, and his chivalry in protecting the child in the grinning teeth of those flashing blades.

At any moment, she knew, that superb body must be hacked to gory ruin, that indomitable and courageous spirit be crushed under Ximchak heels. The thought was an obscenity. It was disgusting.

Behind him, the great Gynosphinx lay helpless. Those strong pinions that had beat against the sky sprawled lax, half-unfolded. The beautiful, unearthly creature, a thing of fabulous legend, had been tumbled ingloriously into the mire by her cowardly, drugged shaft, loosed from ambush. The thought galled her unmercifully. With a shudder of loathing, she let the bow and quiver fall from her hands, and turned to run away from what was happening there in the noisy little clearing under the arching, impersonal branches of the uncaring, placid trees.

But then it was over, or almost. Goaded on by swearing officers swinging whips, wave after wave of Ximchaks sluiced over the corpse-barricade, swinging clubs and cudgels. The brawny little bowlegged man swarmed over the Tigerman and the bronze colossus like vermin. Bludgeons smashed against the furry skull of Grrff, driving him groggily to his knees. Eyes glazing, pink tongue lolling, he sagged and slumped and vanished under a wave of snarling, mad-eyed savages, kicking, pummeling, clubbing.

Ganelon, too, went down under a wave of struggling Ximchaks. Then, like a mighty stag pulled down by yapping hounds, who ventures all on one last magnificent burst of vigor, his bronze form burst free. Ximchaks clung to his neck, his arms, his torso, like furry leeches. He ripped them off his body and flung them from him. One flapped through the air to *splatt* against a tree trunk like a red, wet, overripe fruit. Another thudded into the underbrush, squealing with a snapped spine. His balled fists swinging like bronze mauls, he battered men left and right, and each terrific blow broke a jaw, a head, a shoulder, crushed a mouthful of teeth, squashed an eye to slimy spatterings.

Then he went down, battered to his knees. And this time he was long in staggering to his feet, and the glistening bronze of his brawny torso ran blood from innumerable cuts and bruises. He was still killing Ximchaks, with his bare hands, now, when Ruzara caught her last glimpse of him.

For suddenly a vast black shadow blotted out the sun and drowned the clearing in gloom. Something unthinkably enormous, unthinkably heavy, came inexorably down through snapping branches and toppling trees, to crush half a thousand Ximchaks into pulp beneath its incredible weight.

"Well, at last!" gasped Palensus Choy, as the vast thing rose and settled again on many Ximchaks. For it was Zaradon.

26.

Wolf Turgo Suggests

Puffing and blowing like a winded walrus, Ollub Vetch craned his neck to see things clearly in the huge scrying-crystal. The inky shadow of the Flying Castle blotted out his view below, but through the murk he caught glimpses of yowling chaos as wild-eyed Ximchaks burst in all directions, frenzied to get out from underneath the ponderous-ness of Zaradon.

He caught a glimpse of Ishgadara's mighty form, sprawled out limply, either unconscious or dead. Too risky, trying to set the castle down in the middle of the forest; might squash his friends—if any of them were still alive, that is! Chewing on the ends of his mustaches in an agony of self-accusation, the fat little inventor implored for the eighty-ninth time his laziness. Why, oh, *why*, had it taken him twelve days before getting up the gumption to go looking for his friends? When they hadn't returned to Mount Naroob after the first three days or so, he should have gotten alarmed and worried enough to start out looking for them!

It was those dratted experiments, of course, growled the guilty inventor, swabbing a bald, perspiring brow. Day after day in the lab, toiling over test tubes, puttering around retorts, lost in the fascination of rediscovering lost secrets.

And when he finally *had* gotten worried enough to come looking for his friends, of course, there had been the problem of trying to figure out how Choy made the castle fly. *That* had not been an easy one, either!

Well, late or not, he was here now, was Ollub Vetch; and just in the notorious nick o' time, too, it seemed. For Ganelon Silvermane had been going down for the third time when, skimming the treetops, Vetch had caught a glimpse of turmoil and confusion beneath the trees, and lowered the castle to investigate.

Now he sent the castle up, up, up; then he hovered, making the crystal rotate with the foot pedals, drinking in the swinging panorama of dizzy plains sweeping by, as Ximchaks went scampering from the Urrach grove in all directions at once.

Slapping the levers vengefully, he set Zaradon down on one particularly large tangle of fleeing Ximchaks with a thump that rattled every piece of crockery in the galley. Then he drifted the castle over to that big, busy camp on the seashore he had glimpsed when flying over, and lowered the castle *bump—bump—thump*. Like some ponderous hammer of the Gods the fifty thousand tons of masonry came down on milling mobs and panicking regiments, and when it lifted the better part of a thousand Barbarians had been pounded into the meadow, leaving a gluey smear and not much else.

Before the world was half an hour older, the Ximchaks were in full retreat, pouring back across the plains and splashing through the Wryneck ford, and heading for the Marjid Pass as though thirty million red-hot devils were singeing their very heels. Ollub Vetch maneuvered the Flying Castle recklessly, hovering over the tides of retreating savages, who by now devoutly wished the honor of whelming Trancore had fallen on another clan.

He brought the castle down, squashing them to jelly, and with each descent three or four hundred more Ximchaks bought a farm. It was an uncanny thing to see; and to *hear*. One moment the welkin rang with full-throated choruses of screams, curses, cries, as an immense shadow fell over hundreds of scared, upturned faces—these shriekings rose to a defeaning crescendo as Zaradon came down—then all sound was cut off in a single moment, and there was only silence.

Silence, and a huge square depression stamped deep in the earth, looking damp and sticky.

Before he sickened of the grisly sport, the fat inventor had lowered the Flying Castle twenty-three times.

More than eight thousand Ximchaks never came back from the Ovarva Plains.

Settling to rest on the slopes leading up to the edge of the Urrach, Ollub Vetch scampered into the brush with Chongrilar clumping anxiously at his heels. The Stone Man clenched in one granite fist a bronze bar nine feet long, just in case there were any Ximchaks left in the woods. If there were, they had all of the fight frightened out of them by now, for they encountered nothing that lived or moved until they entered the clearing where bodies were heaped high about the bronze giant.

Ganelon was still alive, although groggy and rubbery in the knees, and so was Kurdi. The giant man had absorbed enough punishment to put six men in the hospital for a month, but his stamina and vitality were many times superior to that of any other man alive on Old Earth, and, surprisingly, he had taken no serious injury. This was probably because the Time Gods had designed him well. His flesh was denser by many times than that of ordinary men, his hide like leather. And such were his recuperative powers that the cuts he had taken were already closing, his bruises and contusions healing visibly.

Kurdi was red with blood from nape to toes, but it was the blood of Ximchaks, happily. The little boy had been half frightened out of his wits, but that had not prevented him from snatching a hooked knife from out of the slowly uncurling fingers of a hand severed from a Ximchak wrist, and with the blade, creeping through the forest of legs on his hands and knees, the brave boy had hamstrung or gutted nine Ximchaks all by himself. Ganelon was so moved by this feat that when he realized it he swept the weary child into his arms and hugged him to his breast wordlessly.

Choy was buried under corpses, and considerably dirtied thereby, but unharmed. Indeed, the Immortal could not suffer bodily injury from any but magical weaponry, and he had fought on to the last. His ivory wand was limp and impotent, but he confessed himself so sick of making lightning that he could easily go a millennium without blasting anything again.

They did not find Grrff.

Or Ishgadara.

They returned to Zaradon, where it perched, slightly at an angle, in the meadow, and soaked the weariness out of themselves in hot baths, ate a huge meal, rested, and talked somberly.

Using his scrying-glass in tandem with his astral vision, Palensus Choy searched the entirety of the Ovarva Plains, at length, before sundown, reporting the discouring news.

Neither Grrff nor the sphinx-girl were anywhere at all in Trancore, either dead or alive, insofar as the magical powers of the Immortal were able to discern.

"What does it mean, magister?" asked Ganelon troubledly.

Choy shrugged dispiritedly.

"I deduce that the Ximchaks retreated in somewhat better order than any of us could have guessed," said the old magician gloomily. "Or some of them did, at least. For one reason or another, they carried off the bodies of our dear friends— if they were slain—or captured them and marched them off over the mountains as prisoners of war—if they yet live. I confess myself surprised at this presence of mind, under the conditions that were prevalent at the time. A leader or two must have survived the massacre, obviously. The ordinary ruffians wouldn't have bothered with prisoners."

"But *why?*" asked Ganelon.

"For insurance, probably," sighed Choy. "We can't very well invade Gompland, not even with the Flying Castle, so long as our dear friends are hostages."

That evening Wolf Turgo sought out Ganelon, where he paced the parapets, unable to compose himself for slumber.

"I have a suggestion for you, big fellow," said the young Ximchak in a subdued voice.

"What is it?"

"You worry about the Tigerman and the winged lion-lady, I know. You can't move against the Horde with this Flying Castle, not if you think they'll butcher your pals if you do. And they will, you know. But there remains one way you can get into Gompland without your friends suffering for it, and once there, who knows what you might be able to do to help free them? I make no promises, mind; no favors; I'm not coming over to your side. But it you enter Gompland as I suggest, it'll help me get back in Zaar's good graces, and maybe you can get your friends free. Remember, I said *maybe.*"

"All right, how can I get into Gompland without—without—" The words stuck in Ganelon's throat and he couldn't speak them.

"Alone—unarmed—helpless—in chains," said Wolf Turgo quietly. "As my prisoner."

There was a long silence.

"Think it over," said Wolf.

Then he turned away, leaving Ganelon Silvermane alone with his thoughts.

They were black and grim and heavy, those thoughts. As black and grim and heavy as the heart within his breast, where hopelessness reigned. Let us be tactful, too, like Wolf Turgo, and leave him alone with his thoughts, and the decision only he could make.

27.

Ganelon Silvermane Decides

The next morning a lone Ximchak appeared on the seashore, waving a sky-blue flag back and forth, in token of parley under truce. Ganelon and Palensus Choy rowed over in one of the fishing boats to see what he wanted.

Eyeing them with a peculiar mixture of apprehension and belligerence, he gruffly announced what they already knew—that Grrff the Xombolian and Ishgadara the sphinx-girl had been captured alive after the Urrach massacre and had been carried away in chains over the Embosch Mountains into the country of the Gomps.

"If'n yer ivver wanna see um alive agin," grinned the other nastily, revealing the rotting stumps of broken teeth, *"an'* in one piece," he added meaningfully, "yew'd better see as how thet thar flyin' fortress o' yourn stay right whar hit be! 'Cause, if'n yew fly hit over inta Gompery, an' try ta squash any more of un, we-uns gonna dew this-and-that."

He proceeded to describe with gloating relish what would be done to the helpless Tigerman and the "lady lion," as he called Ishgadara. He elaborated with gruesome detail for a time. Choy turned pale, gulped, and began to wish his breakfast had not been such a hearty one. Ganelon looked stony, but the pulses were throbbing in his temples and he had trouble breathing because of the lump of raw fury lodged in his throat and choking him.

As he had never before wished for anything in his life, he hungered for the distinct pleasure of pulling the ears off this Ximchak lout and making him eat them. But he held his anger back and heard the man out.

When he had run out of discomforts and indignities to describe, the Ximchak lamely fell silent, scowling truculently,

152

and perspiring a little. The bearers of bad tidings oftentimes come to sticky ends, he knew, and Ganelon looked grim as Death.

"We understand," the bronze giant said stonily. "The castle stays where it is. We shall not invade your camps in Gompland. Anything else?"

"Yeah. If Wolf Turgo ain' bin kilt, let um go," growled the Ximchak. Then he climbed back on his ornith and made tracks for home while Ganelon and Palensus Choy returned in silence to Trancore, each busy with his own thoughts.

Winter had come to Greater Zuavia. It was crisp and cold that morning, and around midday snow flurries fell from a leaden, cloud-heavy sky.

The Trancorians, oblivious to these events, went about their business, leaving the adventurers alone. Choy had explained to the Gray Dynasts that the Ximchak invasion had been stopped, and the Hordesmen had retreated into the Gompish country, and would not return. The solemn counselors somehow managed to convey these happy reports to their idiot monarch, who ennobled Ganelon and his companions with Trancorian baronies. The titles were honorary, although the Emperor Scaviolis was unaware of this fact, the lands and castles bestowed upon the visitors having ages before been submerged beneath the Pommernarian Sea.

Silvermane said nothing, merely nodded, when the bestowal was announced in lofty and flowery language. He reflected sourly on the fact that in the slightly more than three months since he had left behind the safety of his master's enchanted palace of Nerelon and started forth on the seemingly endless road of adventure, he had been unwillingly collecting titles.

He was by now, he mused, Hero of Uth, Defender of Kan Zar Kan, Knight Valardine, and Baron of Trancore. And much good it had done him! He was still faced with the most difficult decision any man can be asked to make.

By nightfall he was gone.

Kurdi came crying to Palensus Choy, holding in one grubby hand a letter scrawled carefully with large, untidy characters.

Choy exchanged a long, thoughtful look with Ollub Vetch, then bent to study the illiterate missive. It was not particularly easy to decipher Ganelon Silvermane's handwriting, because while the same language—Gondwanish—is spoken the length and breadth of the Supercontinent, the orthography differs markedly from one conglomerate to another. Ganelon had been raised in Zermish, a city of the Hegemony, and they spelled things oddly there, at least to the taste of a Zuavian.

But he made it out in time.

Dear Kurdi and All:

I have decided to do what Wolf Turgo suggests. I don't know whether or not I can do anything to help Grrff and Ishy, but the least I can do is try.

I know that they would do the same for me, if things were the other way around.

I am taking the Silver Sword with me, or anyway Wolf Turgo is.

This is goodbye.

I hope that Master Choy and Master Vetch will take good care of you Kurdi. I am leaving you in their care. I hope they will bring you up right, and teach you how to read, and to grow up and be a man. I hope you will be a good boy and not give them any bother.

I know you will be all right, with them to look after you.

I am sorry that things have to end like this.

I hope that Master Choy will try to get word of what has happened back to my master, the Illusionist of Nerelon, who lives in the Crystal Mountains. Please try, anyway. And if he thinks it's the right thing to do, leave it up to him to tell my mother and father what has become of me. Maybe it's better that they don't know, so they won't worry about me. But I will leave this up to him. In case you can't get a letter to the Illusionist, my father is Phlesco the Godmaker. He lives in the Hegemony, in Zermish, on the Street of the Godmakers. He is a member of the House of Forty, and a Burgess.

I love you Kurdi. Be a good boy and do what Master Choy and Master Vetch tell you and try not to get into mischief. Grow up big and strong and brave.

Goodbye to all.

Your friend,

GANELON PHLESCOSSON, CALLED SILVERMANE.

Well, it was quite a letter. Probably the longest letter that Ganelon Silvermane had ever written, and quite possibly the first and only such.

When he was through reading it, Palensus Choy set it down very gently and wiped his eyes with a handkerchief, where just a trace of suspicious moisture could be discerned. Suddenly, for the first time, he looked tired and old.

Ollub Vetch took out a red bandana and honked into it, and wiped his nose for a while, muttering to himself.

Kurdi said nothing, and the look on his face was not the sort of expression that should be seen on the face of one quite so young as he. After a while he got up and wandered listlessly out to be alone for a while.

The two old men looked at one another wordlessly, saying nothing because there wasn't anything to say.

The days got colder and more snow fell until the hideous scars which the Flying Castle had inflicted upon the Ovarva Plains were hidden beneath a white mantle.

Ice formed on the Greater Pommernarian Sea.

Every day Palensus Choy looked into the big scrying-crystal in the observation at Zaradon, which still sat, slightly tilted, on the meadows before the edges of the Urrach.

He caught glimpses of Ganelon Silvermane riding across the Embosch Mountains, ringed about with the warriors in the retinue of Wolf Turgo.

His mighty torso was loaded with heavy chains and he sat astride an ornith. Turgo carried the Silver Sword strapped across his shoulders. Ganelon did not look happy, but neither did he look unhappy. As usual, his expression was inscrutable.

They rode through the Marjid Pass into Gompland and entered the gates of a city called Bernille, where a Ximchak garrison guarded this approach to Gompery.

After that, Choy looked no longer into the crystal. He didn't have the heart to watch what happened.

One night, while a gusty wind yowled around the walls of Zaradon, he and Vetch sipped mugs of hot chocolate, toasting their toes before the roaring firepit.

"D'you think he'll ever come back?" asked the fat inventor after a long silence. There was no need to specify whom he meant by "he."

After a long time Palensus Choy said, very softly:

"No, I don't think so."

Nor did he.

THE APPENDIX

A GLOSSARY OF PLACES MENTIONED IN THE TEXT

Note: The following Glossary includes both natural features, such as forests, mountains, rivers, deserts, and seas, and also man-made features or political divisions, such as city-states, kingdoms, and larger regional units. The numerical designation after each entry refers the reader back to the principal passage or scene in the text of the first three books of the Epic which deals with the place under discussion. The Roman numerals I, II, and III refer to the volume in which the place-name figures prominently, or is first mentioned; "I," therefore, stands for the First Book, *The Warrior of World's End,* "II" for *The Enchantress of World's End,* "III" for the present book, *The Immortal of World's End.* The Arabic numeral which follows the Roman identifies the specific chapter in which the name occurs.

ABBERGATHY. A city of Northern YamaYamaLand situated between the Crystal Mountains and the Voormish Desert. The Indigons would probably have demolished it if they hadn't gone east into the Hegemony instead. I, 4.

AIR MINES. The Air Mines of Karjixia are tunneled into the northern slopes of the Thazarian Mountains; there the Tigermen mined the deposits of frozen oxygen from a buried comet's head rather than pay the exorbitant Air Tax demanded by the Sky Islanders. I, 18.

AOPHARZ. Birthplace of Calidondarius, who saved the Thirtieth Empire of Grand Velademar from destruction. He was the only other Construct to emerge from a Time Vault, and did so ages before Ganelon Silvermane. I, 10.

APHELIS. Easternmost of the nine cities of the Hegemony. I, 3.

ARBALON. Largest of the Seven Inland Seas of Gondwane, located in the southwestern quarter of the Supercontinent. III, 18.

ARDELIX. A ruined city at the southern extremity of the Crystal Mountains, formerly inhabited by a race known as the Hybrids of Phex. Beneath these ruins lay the Time Vault from which Ganelon Silvermane emerged. I, 1.

BARCHEMISH. A realm in the farther parts of Southern YamaYamaLand. Zermishmen traded with it occasionally. I, 3.

THE BARRENS. A hostile wilderness or desert region immediately south of the Crystal Mountains, littered with enormous crystals and from time to time swept by the Blue Rains. I, 1.

BELDOSSA. A small, friendly peaceable country west of Nimboland in Greater Zuavia. III, 9.

BERNILLE. One of the Thirty Cities of the Gompish Regime in Greater Zuavia, just beyond the Marjid Pass. III, 26.

CAOSTRO. A region in Southern YamaYamaLand also known as the Land of the Dead Cities; Chuu, the Kakkawakka Islands, and the Sea of Zelphodon are situated there. I, 3.

CARTHAZIAN MOUNTAINS. A great range which extends due north and exactly from east to west above the Purple Plains, forming a natural border for Greater Zuavia. III, 4.

CHAM ARCHIPELAGO. A chain of islands in the extreme southwestern corner of Gondwane, whose principal island is called Thoph. The archipelago was formerly the home of the Red Amazons, a race now believed extinct, save for Zelmarine the Red Enchantress, who came from there by means of the Halfworld Labyrinth. II, 8.

CHAM EMPIRE. A country of Northern YamaYamaLand due north of the Land of Red Magic and bordering on the Glass Sea. II, *Appendix:* "Red Amazons."

CHUU. A country in Caostro on the northern shores of the Sea of Zelphodon, famous for its Pseudowomen, a form of animals and sentient vegetation almost precisely duplicating the human female. I, 2.

CRYSTAL MOUNTAINS. A range in Northern YamaYamaLand between the Hegemony and Urimadon, consisting of immense masses of rock crystal cloven into prism shapes. Ardelix is situated at the western end of the range and Nerelon at the eastern terminus. I, 1.

DEATH ZONE. An artificially controlled vacuum-bubble in Karjixia, for a time under the influence of Sky Island. I, 18.

DIRDANX. A city in Quentland where the Fabricators of Dirdanx flourished in bygone days. The nembalim, a flying machine used by the Illusionist, was of their workmanship. I, 9.

DOMINIONS OF AKOOB KHAN. A region of barren steppes north and east of the Hegemony where the Black Nomads wander. Ganelon visits this region in the Seventh Book of the Epic. II, 9.

DORAAD. A town in Karjixia threatened by the Airmasters. I, 19.

DROOM. A mountain which is believed the tallest in the Crystal range. There Ganelon Silvermane saved the Illusionist from a pack of yerxels. I, 12.

DWARFLAND. The Country of the Death Dwarves, next to the Land of Red Magic and north of the Hegemony. A bleak, mountainous, inhospitable region inhabited largely by a repulsive species of Antilife. II, 7 (and elsewhere).

EMBOSCH CITY. A border city in the Gompish Regime of Greater Zuavia, demolished by the Ximchak Barbarians. III, 18.

EMBOSCH MOUNTAINS. A range which runs from south to north, forming a natural border between the Gomp country to the east and the Trancorian Empire to the west. Its highest peak, Thunder Troll Mountain, is in the exact same latitude as Island Trancore. III, 18.

ENTHERDY. A small merchant city west of Abbergathy, on the edge of Urimadon. I, 4.

ERIUM. Either a large landlocked bay or one of the Seven Inland Seas near the northern coast of the Supercontinent. III, 18.

FARJ. A region in the northwestern quarter of Gondwane in which the Urghazkoy Horde first rose before the beginning of the Green Jehad. I, 10.

FARZOOL. One of the Thirty Cities of the Gompish Regime, west of the capital.

THE FREE CITY OF CHX. An independent city-state situated between Ning and Poy, directly north of Dwarfland, dominated by the Ethical Triumvirs. II, 1-7.

FROYNOX. Star visible from Gondwane, presumed original home of the Illusionist in his first incarnation. Most commentaries on the Epic regard the account as purely fabulous. I, 11.

GARONGALAND. One of the jungle countries in Southern YamaYamaLand south of the Smoking Mountains, circumjacent to Mount Ziphphiz. I, 3.

GOMPISH REGIME. An immense, million-year-old, enormously populous and wealthy plutocratic empire in Greater Zuavia northwest of the Iriboth Mountains, ruled by thirty dynastic lines of male or female plutocrats, called Regulus or Regina, with an over-plutocrat known as the Regulus Plutarchus. The Gomp race worships wealth, and over the one thousand millennia of their Regime they accumulated a vast superfluity of it. They were conquered almost without resistance, by the irresistible Ximchak Horde, since they maintained no standing army, although each of the Thirty Cities supported a civic militia. Secure behind their presumably impassable mountains they bilked merchants for ages of "passage fees," since they completely controlled the Nine Passes which had always been considered the only means whereby to enter their sequestered realm.

GONDWANE THE GREAT. Old Earth's last and greatest continent which came into existence during the Evening of Time and which remained the central landmass of the planet throughout the Twilight of Time. The last home of man. The Supercontinent comprises the entirety of the former several continents which, according to the Continental Drift Theory, began in the Morning of Time as one enormous landmass (called Pangaea), and which was reformed during the Last Eons. Its land surface consisted of some sixty million square miles, and housed no fewer than one hundred and thirty-seven thousand kingdoms, empires, city-states, federations, theocracies, tyrannies, conglomerates, pseudo-anarchistic anti-states, plutocracies, nations, unions, principates, democracies, oligarchies, cultic or religious occult communities, realms, republics, and other sorts of countries, some for which no conceivable equivalent exists in our language. It was quite a place. I, II, III, *in toto.*

GOROMÉ. Southernmost of the nine cities of the Hegemony. In the Land of Red Magic, for some inexplicable reason, known as "Gorombë." *See* I, 3 and II, 14. The difference between the form of the city's name in the first two books is right there in the next, and is not the error of the redactor.

GLASS SEA. An immense sealike area, larger than the entire country of Ning, consisting of slick, glittering glass, as the name implies. The Savants of Nembosch speculate that the sea was originally a flat region or sandy desert, fused into solid glass by the heat of the friction caused when the comet whose frozen head the Karjixians later mined grazed the surface of Old Earth before plunging deep into the roots of the Thazarian Mountains. See *Air Mines* and II, 5, where it is mistakenly referred to as "the Glass Lake."

GRAND PHESION. Former capital of the Technological Empire of Vandalex in the east-central parts of Gondwane. Ganelon Silvermane does not visit this region until Book Eight, but the City of Technarchs is mentioned throughout the early books, hence this entry.

GRAND VELADEMAR. The city which housed the Thirtieth Empire, consisting of the last remnants of the human race, which was saved by the Thinker of Aopharz. Calidondarius, like Ganelon Silvermane, a Construct sent by the Time Gods. I, 8.

GREAT VELADON. A city on the coast of the Sea of Zelphodon situated at the confluence of the Zelphus River and Thundermountain Falls. Notable chiefly for being the site of the College of the Sacred Sciences and Divinatory Arts known as Ridonga. I, 3.

HARBANAY. One of the Thirty Cities, in the southern part of Gompland. III, 18.

THE HEGEMONY. Or the Realm of the Nine Hegemons. A confederation of nine independent city-states northeast of the Crystal Mountains, composed of Zermish, Oryx, Nambaloth, Jargo, Sabdon, Aphelis, Iblix, Goromé and Pergamoy. Ganelon Silvermane lived some two and a half years in the Hegemonic city of Zermish with his foster-parents. Oryx, in the center, is considered the capital of the Hegemony; there the Hegemonic Council, composed of the nine heriditary rulers of the city-state meets regularly. I, 3-7.

HOLY HORX. A theocratic city-state east of Karjixia and north of Dwarfland. Known to its inhabitants as the City Holy to Gulnazphaz, a god whose Archtemple, situated in that city, was considered one of the Seventy Wonders, it was the center of the Horxite Faith (also known as the Horxite Heresy). I, 16-17.

HORROY. A city west of the Crystal Mountains. I, 4.

IBLIX. A city in the southeastern corner of the Hegemony. I, 3.

IRIBOTH MOUNTAINS. The range due north of Nimboland, forming its natural border. Most prominent of the peaks of this range is Mount Naroob, the site of the famous Flying Castle of Zaradon. III, 9, etc.

IXLAND. A nation in Northern YamaYamaLand, between Holy Horx to the south and Quay to the north. I, 4, etc.

JARGO. A city in the northern parts of the Hegemony. I, 3.

JASHP. A country bordering on the Purple Plains, east of Yombok. There Eshgol the Revealer founded the religion of Jashpianity, whose ecclesiarchs were called the Zealots of Jashp. Extinct in their own homeland, a remnant or two of the Zealots lingered on as wandering bands of migrant evangelists. One such band for a time resided in the Mobile City of Kan Zar Kan, before the Iomagoths. I, 11.

JEMMERDY. A small kingdom on the borders of Northern YamaYamaLand, home of the Siricia, or girl knights of Jemmerdy, as Xarda, for example. The capital is called Vladium. I, 20.

JURAGO. Chief city and capital of the Gompish Regime, held by the Warlord of the Ximchaks after the Horde conquered the Thirty Cities and disthroned Tharzash the Last Regulus. III, 21.

(To Be Continued)